# The Kilminster Diaries

# THE KILMINSTER DIARIES

## A MURDER MYSTERY

Henry Averns

Published by Iguana Books



Publisher: Cheryl Hawley
Editor: Michael Carroll

ISBN 978-1-77180-763-0 (paperback)
ISBN 978-1-77180-762-3 (epub)

This is an original print edition of *The Kilminster Diaries*.

*This novel is dedicated to Catherine Standish — you know who you are. And to Ernie, Stan, and Arthur, the best friends anybody could ask for, who hopefully will spend their eternity chasing balls and swimming in lakes.*

# CONTENTS

To be honest as this world goes is to be one man picked out of ten thousand.

— William Shakespeare, *Hamlet*, act 2, scene 2

**Balthasar:**

Sigh no more, ladies, sigh no more,

Men were deceivers ever,

One foot in sea, and one on shore,

To one thing constant never.

Then sigh not so, but let them go,

And be you blithe and bonny,

Converting all your sounds of woe

Into hey nonny nonny.

— William Shakespeare, *Much Ado About Nothing*, act 2, scene 3

# Prologue

## Divorce, the Future Tense of Marry

### August 27, 2004

Dr. Richard Headley was holding a piece of toast in one hand as he opened the front door of his large five-bedroom executive home to receive the recorded delivery letter. To sign for it, he was forced to hold the toast between his teeth, causing a chunk of orange marmalade to slip off onto the sleeve of his peacock-blue silk dressing gown.

Richard had received a few letters like this before — usually invitations for medico-legal work. He recognized the name of the lawyer on the back of the envelope. Money for nothing as a rule. Smiling, he thought about how a good cardiology medico-legal case might help him get closer to buying that new Audi coupe he'd been eyeing.

He threw the envelope onto the quartz counter near the toaster where it sat for the rest of the day and for the next four days until enough letters had accumulated for him to feel the energy involved in opening them was justified. Thus, it was late afternoon on Friday when he sat in his kitchen with a lonely bottle of Pinot Noir and a single wineglass to deal with his mail.

Richard was already feeling marginally aggrieved that his wife had decided a few days ago to travel to Belgium with a friend and hadn't even prepared him any meals to consume during her absence. Since he had no idea where the saucepans were kept, he elected to drive into town for fish and chips from the Silver Cod. But first he attended to the mail, which turned out to be four bills, a flyer for free roof insulation, an invitation to join an online wine club, and an application for divorce from his wife.

His reactions included slight indignation, since this was the second time this had happened, shortly followed by greater annoyance that she hadn't warned him about the letter, then an overwhelming feeling of anxiety that he would soon be joining the twenty-five percent club. Richard was already paying fifty percent of his income to his ex-wife. Fifty percent wasted just because she couldn't forgive him for the two or three affairs that she knew about.

The house had been remortgaged twice to pay for three children to fail to complete degrees. They'd been at a prestigious prep school followed by boarding from the ages of eleven to eighteen at Winchester College. The total investment in his progeny could have bought a holiday home in Provence. The oldest was now somewhere in Thailand shadowing Richard's copulatory footsteps, the next had dropped out of law school after two years to become a juggler, and the third, the brightest, was living in a motorhome in Brighton, earning enough to live by milking the benefits system efficiently.

He paid his ex-wife — his first ex-wife, she'd now be called — a substantial monthly allowance. Richard rapidly calculated his net worth on the back of the envelope from his wife's lawyer. Probably eight hundred thousand. He halved it. Four hundred thousand. He took off the value of the mortgage, which he'd forgotten to consider in his first net-worth calculation. Four hundred and fifty thousand. He took off the lease payments on the current Audi. Apparently, his net worth was less than nothing. At that point, he balled up the envelope and threw it at the dog, which assumed this was a game and brought it back, leaving it on Richard's lap.

It was quite clear that he had three choices. First, work for two ex-wives and live off a substantially reduced pension until the blessed relief of death. Second, choose wife number three from a small pool of available women with assets. Or third, arrange for his current wife to die unexpectedly.

Being a man who thought ahead, Richard didn't perform an internet search on ways to remove an unwanted appendage. He'd read about fools who did that from their homes, so he'd save that for a trip to the hospital library.

He was already feeling marginally better, and the project began in earnest.

Richard peered at himself in the mirror as he walked from the kitchen to the living room, a bottle in one hand, his almost-empty first glass in the other. *Still pretty attractive*, he mused. He noticed some loose skin hanging under his chin, which he tried to smooth back into place. Remembering his paunch, he sucked it in. And there were increasing streaks of grey in his still-fine hair. He'd get that attended to before anything else.

*Yes,* he thought. *I'm still quite a catch.*

Which begged the question: Why had he had twenty-six relationships, none of which had succeeded? One thing he knew for certain. It wasn't because of him.

Twenty-six unreasonable women, two episodes of chlamydia, one of gonorrhea, and several hundred thousand pounds. His accountant had once asked him if he'd ever paid for sex. Richard's immediate answer had been no, but as he stared at the dog ripping up the lawyer's envelope, he realized that, yes, he *had* paid for sex.

On the same day Dr. Headley received his financially inconvenient news, another adventure was evolving, this time involving Darren Greanleaf. He, too, had had his fair share of misfortune.

Darren could easily have been Idris Elba — just as tall, just as black, and just as handsome. He could have been a great actor like Idris but had lacked the motivation to study, and without any qualifications other than looking very cool and very tough, he'd secured a job as a guard at a high-end jeweller in Bristol.

On the very infrequent days when a customer entered the shop, Darren seemed invisible to them. By the end of each day, his shoes were so tight he dared not take them off until he was home, otherwise they'd never go back on.

He spent two years, three months, and five days standing by the front door in a dark suit, the better to deter potential thieves. All day long he dreamed of Hollywood and another thousand careers that fate had denied him — aided by a lack of motivation, he admitted to himself. Darren found the job mind-numbingly dull. Despite a lack of objective qualifications, he was a bright man with an IQ higher than anybody else in the store.

"If only you could apply yourself, like Dennis," his mother told him each night when he came home and sat in the kitchen where his dinner was waiting in the oven. Dennis was his brother, a pharmaceutical representative, better known as a drug rep. His brother had the gift of charm and had schmoozed through life with a company car and an enviable income.

On the day he reached two years, three months, and six days of work at the jeweller's, at five o'clock in the afternoon — the same day and time Dr. Headley was cursing his rotten luck and sipping a glass of wine, Darren went for a pee. In the two minutes he was away, the store was robbed and Darren missed the first chance in his life to shine. Every tray of rings on display was taken by a pair of armed robbers in a very efficient heist lasting ninety seconds.

Naturally, being Black, Darren was immediately suspected of complicity in the crime, and while charges were never brought, he was laid off from the role on the same day as the robbery at exactly the same time as Catherine's brother, veterinarian Ian Beaney, received written confirmation of suspension by his regulatory body.

The reader may be forgiven for being unaware that Catherine Standish is the wife of Brian, whose memoirs ensue in this book. Ian, the vet, had initially been suspended after the unfortunate accidental euthanizing of a spaniel that had come in for a routine procedure. His sin, in the eyes of his regulatory body, was compounded by sending an invoice to the unfortunate owner. There had been further complaints considered, many related to overcharging clients. Always happy to live beyond his means, Beaney chose to cope with this financial disaster by buying some platinum earrings for his wife.

Darren had been laid off from his job in full public view, and as he followed the direction to "bloody well leave and never return," one of the rare customers hurried out after him with an offer he couldn't refuse. The customer explained that the job simply entailed boarding an EasyJet flight to Nice, taking a taxi to a local farm, picking up a sample of racehorse semen, and bringing it back in a small, insulated cup where he would pass it on at a petrol station a mile after leaving Bristol's airport.

On the day the vet was suspended, when Darren was offered the new job, while Richard Headley's net wealth was reduced further, Dr. Brian Standish was sitting at his desk having once again returned to Kilminster Hospital, blissfully unaware that these separate events were hurtling to a meeting point. That meeting point was to be Brian's office.

# 1

# JAILBIRD

## DECEMBER 17, 2004

I was in a jail cell in Kilminster writing in my diary, having gone from pillar of the community to murder suspect in the space of a few hours. I could still see the excited faces of my colleagues as they rushed to get a glimpse of me being whisked through the main entrance of my hospital to a police car, lights flashing. When I glimpsed the appalled expressions of some of my fickle friends, I realized they were likely gossiping and speculating about how they'd always known I was a little odd. I could hear them saying, "A bit of a loner. No — just an antisocial bastard. Yes, it's always the quiet ones who commit murder."

Before long, they'd probably link me to the death of Colin Marks, who was found a couple of years back with a colonoscope up to the hilt, his mackerel eye staring at the screen where his final image in life would have been a small colonic polyp. This had all been forgotten about until a local medium recently claimed to be in touch with him "on the other side." She was interviewed by the local newspaper, insisting that Colin was murdered and didn't simply have a heart attack as recorded on his death certificate.

I was arrested for a different crime, though: the slaying of a young male nurse found dead in the hematology treatment room less than twenty-four hours ago, still clutching a Post-it note branded with the name of an anti-thrombotic drug I'd passed to him, telling him to be there after work and to make sure he told nobody.

When Inspector Jock McAlister of the local police presented the evidence of my guilt to me, I'd certainly have believed myself to be the prime suspect, since I'd arranged the meeting and was captured on a hospital camera entering the treatment room around the time of the murder. What was more, one of the nurses overheard me telling the victim he'd be dead soon if he didn't do as I said. And then there was a beer mat with a range of ways to commit murder written in my handwriting now in an evidence bag. So, despite feeling disgruntled, I had some sympathy for the inspector, though I didn't feel handcuffs were called for.

Catherine, my wife, had dropped off a pair of pajamas, a pillow with a Buzz Lightyear pillowcase — one of the children's — and a peanut butter sandwich she'd packed in the My Little Pony lunch box I'd been using for many years but which was the source of considerable mockery from the officers working that evening. I wasn't allowed to eat the sandwich, and sitting here, I recalled the jailer brushing crumbs off his moustache. I'd taken their names and made a mental note that should they ever develop leukemia they'd be smiling on the other side of their faces if they got referred to my department.

The police had offered me a chance to obtain free legal advice. "You can request the duty solicitor to come down this evening."

"Who is it?" I'd asked, not that any name would have meant anything to me.

"I think Geoff Furniss is on tonight."

He was the son of my pervert neighbour up the road. "I'm an innocent man," I'd announced rather dramatically. "I don't need a lawyer."

The officer had raised his eyes to the ceiling and muttered something about an anchor that I couldn't quite hear.

I hadn't even been back at work very long after taking leave since the previous set of Kilminster murders. Indeed, it was difficult for me to work out where this latest twist in the saga began. What I could say was that I admitted to Inspector McAlister I'd planned to meet the deceased at 5:30 yesterday evening. I could hardly deny it, since I'd written it in my diary. Neither could I refute that he would have been somewhat trepidatious, almost certainly knowing the purpose of our meeting.

However, I strenuously denied exsanguinating a human being. I wasn't even sure that was possible. Phlebotomizing seven units of human blood into individual blood bags was certainly quite considerate compared to letting it flow across the floor of our treatment room, but try as I might, I couldn't convince the police officers that the time and effort this entailed wasn't available to me the previous night because I'd been at Kilminster Public Library to find a book on the history of morris dancing, my latest hobby.

I'd asked if they could delay my arrest until the morning, since our club had a guest speaker from the Morris Dancing Federation this evening lecturing on the "Origins of the Dorset Two-Step." The application of handcuffs was answer enough. I'd asked Catherine to go along and take notes, but she'd seemed unwilling.

Catherine had brought in my diary from the past few months, along with a few I kept at medical school, and my plan had been to spend the rest of the night trying to put everything together and somehow convince McAlister to use his imagination and search elsewhere for a different suspect. If I had the time, I might even reflect on how I'd managed to get through medical school and become a hematologist, since I figured my life declined the day I accepted the offer from Bristol Medical School. Or was it when I was doing A-levels and the school asked if I'd choose engineering, law, finance, or medicine, no other career path perhaps being worthy?

While I was thinking about it, I put a written complaint in my diary about the quality of the mattress they'd provided, along with the brusque response from the jailer, though I was a little concerned the prison office might confiscate my pen, a gift from Plus Denario Pharmaceuticals, a small token from the company that had recently been the reason for me to attend a symposium in Munich.

Plus Denario was a rising star in the world of Big Pharma. Readers of my previous memoir would be well aware that I wasn't susceptible to the bribery and corruption of doctors by companies peddling new, generally useless drugs. However, only a fool would have declined the recent invitation of a trip to Munich, site of the firm's research centre, for a two-day educational meeting that included a tour of its research laboratories.

Setting aside my deeply held convictions for two days, I joined a group of eighteen hematologists for the event. I rehearsed the ethical implications with Catherine, who didn't approve but who suspected she'd end up with a gift, so in the end, she encouraged me to go. It only meant sacrificing two days for my personal development, I rationalized. The reality was we'd go to several restaurants, have a good time in multiple bars, and spend minimal time actually working. The marketing teams had obviously figured this would result with us prescribing more of their drug.

Unlike my colleagues, I was pretty sure I wasn't susceptible to this sort of nonsense. When we arrived at the Plus Denario headquarters, we were given the chance of a guided tour through the company's museum where it celebrated its great successes over the previous decades.

Then we were taken to the firm's laboratory where we were excited to hear we'd see a demonstration of the steps involved in developing a drug, specifically a new one for asthma. As we were hustled into the small, somewhat dimly lit laboratory, we were told the company's senior scientist, Dr. Hans Roth, would conduct us through the procedure. While we waited for him, I noticed a cage full of white mice happily scurrying around, oblivious to their impending doom.

A rather dismal-looking man, tall and skeletal with small round wire-framed glasses and a white lab coat, strode straight toward us. Oddly, upon arriving in front of us, he stamped his right foot hard. Without so much as a greeting or smile, he pointed to a glass bell jar on the laboratory bench that had a couple of rubber tubes attached to its top. "Observe ze glass bell jar," he said in a perfect impression of a of an Englishman pretending to speak German. He then slowly donned a pair of gloves.

My colleague to my right, Jane Moore, sniggered.

Dr. Roth stared hard at her. I thought he was going to slap her across the face with his rubber gloves. Instead, he opened the cage, picked up a mouse by its tail, and put it in the bell jar.

"I vill now be squirting ze gas and ze mouse vill die. Observe." He opened a tap on one of the tubes in the top of the bell jar, allowing in some sort of gas. "Zis vill now tighten up ze mouse's airways."

As predicted, the mouse started to shake for about ten seconds and promptly died. For the first time in his performance, the scientist beamed broadly, proud of the presentation so far.

Jane fainted, and two other members of our group attended to her while Dr. Roth proceeded to repeat the experiment with a second mouse from the cage. He went through the whole process again, but this time, as well as giving the noxious gas, he opened a small tap on the second tube, releasing some of the new drug for asthma. Initially, the mouse trembled, then as predicted by Dr. Roth, it recovered, surviving the experiment.

I wasn't sure whether we were meant to clap, cheer, or just nod sagely. I was aware that ten different groups were visiting this department over the next few weeks, and when I glanced back at the white cage, I noted there were twelve mice left to demonstrate the new drug. One of the mice caught my eye, seemingly begging me to smuggle it out of the laboratory.

Next, we were ushered into a lecture hall where we were treated to thirty minutes of propaganda — a small price to pay given the plan was to take us to a bar in town. Generally speaking, going out for a meal with the pharma industry was a chance to eat well, meet colleagues, and have fun. Sadly, on this occasion, I was foolish enough to go for a pee before choosing my seat, and when I returned to the restaurant, I noted with dismay that there was only one seat left. On one side sat a marketing head, Janos Paraskavopoulos, whom I could only assume was Italian from his name, though he just stared at me completely confused when I spoke to him in his mother tongue. He stared discontentedly at the menu, oddly complaining that they had no Greek options. On my other side was

Hans Roth, the mouse-murdering scientist who was equally unhappy with the menu, since there was no Wiener schnitzel. So they both chose British meat pies with mushy peas. It was going to be a long night.

And, indeed, as I sat there in my jail cell, I knew this, too, would be a long night.

# 2

# REINTRODUCING MYSELF

**SEPTEMBER 4, 2004**

My wife, Catherine, would describe me as perceiving life as a half-empty glass. Her actual words: "Brian Standish, you're such a Negative Nancy. I can't believe what a miserable bastard you've become." Or even worse: "You're actually worse than my father."

Her father was, indeed, a true curmudgeon. Even when Catherine and her brother, Ian Beaney, were young, he was the same. I gathered he regularly played hide-and-seek with the children, getting them to hide, then sitting in the living room to read his newspaper in peace.

I tended to agree. Upon careful analysis of most situations, I was quickly able to identify most things that could go wrong. I used to dislike most people. Now I strongly disliked them. There was nothing like a medical staff meeting to remind one that twenty people could sit for an hour and cordially despise one another. Therefore, I saw myself as a cordial misanthropist.

Catherine gave the illusion of friendliness. For example, in Kilminster last week, she was super-friendly in a slightly disturbing manner. In every shop, she beamed at the storekeeper and chatted about the weather, how pretty their dress was, how hard it was to find tinned guava, and such like, always with a big smile.

"When did you become so friendly?" I asked.

"I've always been like this, Brian. I'm friendly to everyone … until I know them. Then I'm more like you."

I used to be a doctor. Well, actually, I still was, though not a night has gone by in the past twenty years when I didn't approach sleep imagining other, better careers I could have chosen. So now I viewed myself as between careers despite carrying on with the first.

I thought I'd left hematology for good. In the previous few years, there was a series of violent murders in my hospital after one of our managers, the late Jeremiah Foch, went on a killing spree. I'd avoided his attempts on my life at least three times before Jeremiah was identified as the culprit.

The truth was that even without Jeremiah I would have searched for a way out of my current job because the combination of conceit, arrogance, racism, sexism, pharma corruption, and intellectually bereft Health Service leaders were hard to stomach. Surprisingly, most of the patients were very likable, probably because knowing I held the key to their survival tilted the relationship in my direction. There would, however, still be at least one patient per day who brought to mind cinder blocks, rope, and large lakes.

An example of a cinder-block-patient scenario went like this:

"Other than night sweats and the lump in your neck," I'd ask, "have you noticed any other new symptoms?"

"Hold on," she'd say, reaching for a bit of paper from her coat pocket and staring at it for twenty seconds. "Yes, I have tingling in my right forearm sometimes."

"Okay, when was the last time that happened?"

"Nineteen ninety-six."

"Mmm … anything else?"

"Yes, sometimes I get heartburn after spicy food."

"Okay," I'd reply, stifling an exasperated grimace and regretting opening this door.

"Sometimes I get brain fog. And if I rush upstairs too fast, I get slightly short of breath. Last week, I dropped a cup. Oh, and there's a sort of buzzing sensation on the outside of my knee."

It might well be that I'd been missing Chronic Powel Syndrome all these years and what I should really have been doing was prescribing the new drug for this condition — Orgasmia, fifteen milligrams daily.

What should I have done instead of a career in medicine? A few colleagues had forged a career in the pharmaceutical industry. However, when I studied any of the Big Pharma companies, it was clear to me from the various fines for price-fixing, false claims, lies over safety data, and other anti-competitive behaviour that I didn't have the unscrupulous nature to survive in the industry.

I think I could have been a good farmer, but not actually possessing a farm had been a deal breaker for that career. Recently, I had a good bash at writing, and my first autobiography, *Fatal Medicine*, sold twelve copies, which likely wouldn't be enough to feed my children. I had eighty copies left in a box in my office at work.

I'd seen a few advertisements for medical jobs in exotic locations and hadn't fully ruled those out. Australia appealed but seemed a little far away from my mother, who had been telling us she was terminally ill for several years now yet still led a robust globe-trotting life: cruises, city breaks, resort holidays, all seemingly with a chain of eligible widowers, each of whom was a cad. More disturbingly, she'd lately begun to enthusiastically infer that their relationships were akin to teenage romance. One must never be forced to imagine one's mother being ridden by a man called Major Percy Clift, who still used his military rank, wore mustard-coloured trousers, and whose false teeth were Dulux brilliant white.

"Don't look so prudish, Brian. I'm not too old to be pleasured" were words no son should have to hear.

Catherine wanted to be close to her own parents, Jack and Winnie, who were currently barely talking to me after a poorly worded bon mot on euthanasia had landed badly. We'd had a further falling-out at the Taj Mahal. Not in India but the more popular destination, a restaurant on Kilminster High Street.

Her father, Jack, as usual, made a considerable fuss about his dyspepsia and insisted he could only have the mild Bengal chicken with boiled rice and therefore wouldn't share food with the rest of us. That was the point where things went wrong.

We ordered some pappadums. Four arrived in a small basket. Jack put two on his plate. When the dishes arrived, Catherine's father sat there with his meal before him. I didn't need reminding that this was Jack's and wasn't to be shared. Actually, I was pleased. The chicken pieces looked like old bones from a previous customer's leftovers. He poked his food around a little, gazing at our lamb rogan josh, beef methi, sag aloo, and prawn bhuna.

I took two small pieces of meat from each dish, as did Catherine and Winnie. "How's your chicken Bengal?" I asked, eyeing the pitiful pile of bones on his plate.

Jack smiled. "I used to go to school with a guy called Ben Gall."

"Really," I said.

"Oh, Brian," sighed Catherine.

In my defence, this wasn't a man one could imagine having a sense of humour. At that point, Jack, who had yet to taste his own meal, throwing caution to the wind as he shoved an antacid between his teeth, reached over for a taste of what he was missing out on.

None of us said a word as he scraped most of our meal onto his plate, commenting that we were wasteful. Oblivious to the fact that we'd each had barely a mouthful, Jack tucked into the mountain of food in front of him and devoured it. I found myself hoping desperately for a perforated stomach ulcer to finish him off.

To add insult to injury, when the bill came, Jack kept a stony silence and refused to look at the black wallet with the white edge of the bill poking out tantalizingly. I managed to sit it out for a good twenty seconds before weakening. Naturally, he didn't offer to share the cost. He did, however, grab three of the four mint chocolate Matchmakers that were enclosed with the reckoning. Once again, I hoped desperately that one of the illegal workers in the back of the restaurant had a case of dysentery to pass on to Jack.

Just to irritate her, I hugged Winnie goodbye. Catherine's mother had always been very cold — not tactile or demonstrative of love. A hug goodbye was somewhat awkward, since she stiffened up and had no idea what to do with her arms. Winnie was even like that with her husband, leading one to wonder how they'd ever managed to breed.

After that evening, things were pretty tense with Catherine's parents. Thus, it was disappointing that my wife didn't see the advantages of crossing a mighty ocean to get a little farther away from them.

Instead, she insisted on organizing family events with them on an annual basis. It was only a year earlier that Catherine had decided we needed to spend quality time with her family. Imagine my delight then to know we were going away for five days with her two sisters and parents, though her brother, Ian, wriggled out of it, saying he was travelling abroad. So, we decided to go to Super Parcs, a curious European invention designed to tear families apart. If ever there was a place reminding one how bad the average human looks in swimwear, it was Super Parcs.

Catherine's father was chronically depressed because he was married to her mother, whose morose manner would undoubtedly place a black cloud over the weekend. I noticed Winnie wore a swimsuit that failed to cover up the required areas, which I suspected resembled last year's hanging baskets.

My wife's older sister was fun … if you were in the mood for gossip. Most conversations started with the words "I don't want to speak ill of anybody, but …" Then she spoke ill of whomever it was currently *de rigueur* to discuss. I could at least relate to her ability to find the worst in most people.

Her younger sister had celiac disease, or so she claimed. It turned out there was something worse than a vegan at a party. While I had every sympathy for people with celiac disease, Polly's ability to constantly steer the conversation back to what foods contained gluten was beginning to wear me down. I struggled to keep silent. Indeed, I was fairly sure the whole thing was a charade, since she'd been in a Pizza Hut the previous week and I'd seen her gorging on a pizza Napoli.

The second morning, we agreed to spend the day relaxing, reading, swimming, and doing what wholesome families do. I headed to the indoor water park.

At the top of the water slide sat a woman who, along with her complete family, had been cruelly touched by the ugly stick. In fact, upon examination, I realized they'd actually gotten completely caught up in the ugly tree. I sat behind her in awe of the terrible tattoos surely done by herself while trying to peer in a mirror. She appeared somewhat unwashed, the soles of her feet black with grime, hair matted and greasy.

Quickly, I determined I didn't wish to share her water. So, I left the pool and made my way to Treasure Cove, the relaxing area where Catherine and her family were sharing two plastic chairs between the five of them, since we'd failed to arrive at dawn to ensure proper seats.

The children at least were enjoying themselves in the lazy river. A moment later, they were asked to leave the water urgently as a child had defecated in the pool. In their urgency to get out, one of the girls slipped on the floor, cutting her chin, which immediately poured blood down her chest and caused a lifeguard to scream at us that she might have hepatitis B and could we leave immediately.

Catherine, upbeat as always, proposed we play badminton. I headed to the event booking zone, but all the courts were taken for the next week. Horse riding would have been fun but was also fully reserved. The small lake with sailing dinghies and canoes was closed, owing to a forecast of lightning that also precluded walking the nature trail around the perimeter of the park. The spa had space tomorrow at nine in the morning.

I suggested we go to the bar, but Catherine's mother vetoed that, so we headed to Pancake House where we were told, "Yes, there's a table for ten. It'll be ready at 3:30." It was eleven o'clock.

Deflated, we headed back to our respective chalets to watch televisions and listen to the rain beat on the roofs.

All of this was why I wanted to leave the country. Instead of an exciting adventure like that, though, Catherine and I remained on the outskirts of Kilminster, living off our savings and her income, which I topped up with a part-time job in a brewery, my responsibility being to propagate the yeast for the brews because I knew how to use a microscope. When my aging Honda Civic required new brakes, fate decreed I'd return full-time to my still-unfilled post in the hematology department of Kilminster Hospital.

Talking of propagating yeast, I'd forged an unlikely friendship with Dr. Richard Headley, cardiologist, philanderer, and narcissist. When I received a text message from him on a Saturday morning in September 2004, asking me to call him immediately, I was quite happy to do so.

"Brian, my friend …" he started.

I was immediately on my guard. Nobody used the phrase "my friend" without the requirement for immediate doubt about that person's sincerity. He was clearly about to ask me an unreasonable favour. "*Wasup?*" I responded, having learned from my children how the modern man should converse.

"We need to meet urgently. Green Dragon, Hobarton, midday."

"What … today?" I stammered. "I'm supposed to take Catherine to get her nails done."

"Cancel it. This is important. And say nothing to anyone, particularly Catherine."

As I put the phone down, Catherine turned to me and asked who it was.

"Richard Headley. He wants to meet me at midday at the Green Dragon. Very mysterious. He told me I mustn't tell you."

"He's probably plotting to kill his wife. She told me she was leaving him. You can hardly blame her, can you? Though God knows how he's put up with her. She has the intellect of an amoeba. Well, maybe you can drop me off in town for my nail appointment and pick me up on your way back."

That was somewhat easier than I'd expected. I was immediately on my guard for the second time in two minutes. Why was she being so reasonable about my meeting a libertine who occupied the moral low ground?

# 3

# The Carpark

## September 4, 2004

On my way to the Green Dragon, I dropped Catherine off in the marketplace, then headed to the supermarket to buy a leg of lamb for tomorrow's Sunday roast. At the meat counter, I bumped into Desmond Leech and enthusiastically wished him good day, but he walked on, pretending not to see me.

Professor Sir Desmond Leech, OBE, was a general surgeon. His knighthood was the reward for inventing a new technique to join the duodenum to another piece of bowel as a pioneering treatment for morbid obesity. Every chair in his clinic waiting room was made from steel girders to accommodate the patients hoping he'd replumb them and allow them to continue to eat yet lose weight and achieve the perfect beach body.

Invariably, he sat on national committees for medical safety, education, training, and such like. He was a regular government adviser for all sorts of issues, most of which I doubt he was qualified to hold an opinion on. But the combination of a title, a plummy accent, and a bow tie made even the most vacuous person reasonably believable.

While highly respected by all staff for his surgical skills, he maintained most nursing and medical staff in a state of high fear. He was conceited, short-tempered, and entitled, and treated everybody as if their roles in the hospital were to serve him.

I gathered that a good reference from him still boosted careers, which was why there remained fierce competition by aspiring surgeons to get a training post on his team. He had a timid wife named Clementine whom he never invited to hospital events. I only knew of her existence because she was one of my patients and spent more of the consultation moaning about Sir Desmond than telling me about her symptoms. She mentioned that he worked on Fridays in London where he ran a private bariatric clinic with no shortage of patients. It was said that upon arrival they entered through extra-wide doors. A few months on, they were likely allowed to slip in through a narrow side entrance to show off their new, chiselled, skinny bodies. His Harley Street private practice was recently in jeopardy, however, after he'd walked out of a consulting room singing "Hey, Fatty Boom Boom," leading to a complaint to the General Medical Council.

As I headed toward the till to pay, I thought I saw Sir Desmond slipping a packet of batteries into his jacket pocket. I'd heard about wealthy people shoplifting and was quite alarmed by what I'd seen but decided on balance I was probably mistaken. This was a man with a Land Rover Discovery, a Porsche, a swimming pool, and an ego the size of the county. He hardly needed to steal a battery.

As a hematologist, I'd occasionally interacted with him, usually to request a splenectomy or a lymph node biopsy, so we knew each other relatively well on a collegiate level. A minute or so later when I emerged with my shopping, I spotted Sir Desmond. He was wandering about the cars with a bad-tempered expression, and I surmised he'd lost his Porsche, because I could see his ridiculous bright red racing car, complete with some sort of fin on the back, behind a transit van. I strolled over to help him, and despite knowing me well, he utterly blanked me. So instead I left him and headed for my Honda Civic. I was fairly sure he even used the "f" word as I ambled off, which just demonstrated that eminence didn't always confer good manners.

# 4

# THE PROPOSAL

## SEPTEMBER 4, 2004

I was a few minutes late. Richard Headley was already sitting at a tall table alone, ready for our mysterious lunchtime meeting, with two pints and an open packet of cheese and onion crisps in front of him.

As always, he had the film-star look about him: full head of hair, chiselled jaw, and a tooth that twinkled with an audible *ping* when he cracked his broad smile. He was wearing a cream sweater with a dark green Barbour gilet, ensuring everybody in the pub understood he was a privately educated and successful man. Headley knew he was good-looking. That was the problem.

I tried to join him by the direct route but became entangled in the extendable leash of a hideously obese Jack Russell terrier attached to a ghastly creature out of a Harry Potter movie and who was utterly oblivious to the mayhem her animal was causing. I guessed she was about forty-five, but a pack-a-day smoking habit had added fifteen years to her. She'd managed to extend this a further five years by employing a toddler to apply her makeup and dying her hair jet-black with a seductive mauve streak on the side. When she scowled at me as if it were my fault the leash had tripped me, I realized this was Wanda Foch, sister of Jeremiah, our late medical department manager. Luckily, she didn't recognize me.

After I was finally perched on the stool opposite Richard, I was keen to learn why we were meeting. "What could possibly require such urgency and subterfuge, Richard?"

He put a finger to his lips and responded *sotto voce*. "I'm writing a book, Brian. And I need to review a few details about the so-called *perfect murder*."

"Are you for real? I thought at least you had cancer or were being fired from work. Or maybe your wife was leaving you …"

Richard shot me a wide-eyed, panicked look and hushed me quickly. "I'm not sure why you'd think that, but as it happens, we're currently going through a tricky period. But that has nothing whatsoever to do with my book."

"So not everything's perfect at home then?"

He gazed over my shoulder at the pub dartboard, a wistful, faraway look in his eyes. The face of a man still in love, perhaps crushed by recent news that such emotion wasn't reciprocated. "She looks like an angel. She has perfect skin, a wonderful smile, beautiful legs. And those sapphire eyes." He seemed utterly smitten by the beauty of his wife.

He continued. "She has endless kindness and patience, but none of it stops me wanting to bludgeon her to death with a blunt object every time I see her. Even when I hear her breathing, she annoys me. I spend most of my time imagining the freedom of life without her. She's just utterly banal. If I want to talk politics, she'll read her horoscope. All she wants to watch on TV is *Britain's Got Talent* or *Coronation Street*. I feel imprisoned by her. But now she's had the audacity to go to a lawyer and ask to divorce *me*! I bet that newspaper mystic suggested it to her. That's the worst of it."

Finished his rant, he took a long sip of beer. The mystic in question was a woman who lived above the Silver Cod, Saffron Brown, who had recently acquired a regular weekly astrology column in the local Kilminster newspaper. Then, as an afterthought, he added, "Plus the fact I'll be as poor as you by the time she's done." He grinned despite himself.

I sympathized with Richard. There was, indeed, something about his wife that could start off endearing and end up excruciatingly annoying. She was both beautiful and stupid. And only one of those would last forever.

When I was a young boy, I remember waking up one evening to the alarming feral sound of two cats mating. My mother told me they were just having a playful fight. Harvey, my brother, said with great delight they were having sex and that the male cat had a barbed penis to stimulate the female to ovulate. Perhaps this was the start of Harvey's long-term obsession with the phallus.

I hadn't given that incident much more thought until the first evening I met Richard Headley's wife. She had somewhat misjudged the amount of gin a woman of one hundred and ten pounds could drink before moving on to wine. When her arms suddenly developed a life of their own, she knocked over her glass of wine across our new tablecloth. With infinite patience and kindness, Richard quietly suggested that perhaps she shouldn't have another drink that evening. To say that wasn't received well would be an understatement. She transformed from petite angel to spitting devil in a dramatic five seconds. After an anal-clenching, bladder-loosening tirade, it was clear she disagreed with Richard's assessment of the situation. Shakily, I poured her a new glass of wine, which lasted approximately ninety seconds before she knocked that one over, too.

Bizarrely, my main memory of the evening was that her voice when angry reminded me precisely of a mating cat. I commiserated with Richard that he'd committed to spend his life with her, though commitment in Headley's mind was a looser arrangement than many would assume.

There was a young woman at the bar who glanced over at our table. With his radar fully functional, Richard recovered from his distress and immediately began a remote-charm offensive, starting with the nonchalant Hollywood smile and raising his glass to her.

"Wow, that one's a beauty, Brian. Look at that facial jewellery. Means she's a wild one. See, I've still got it." He smiled as she raised her glass back at him. "I'm the Lord Byron of Kilminster."

"Wasn't Lord Byron into young boys?" I ventured. That went over his head, since he was already standing up from his chair to make his way over to the next Mrs. Headley.

"Watch and learn, Brian, as I go in search of The Mighty Quim."

Somewhere along his journey Richard had transitioned from charming rake to creepy pest. Lately, his attempts to befriend young junior female doctors had been rebuffed, and one sensed he was teetering on the edge of a complaint in which the whole house of cards would fall.

He made his way to the bar as if to buy another round. I watched him turn to the lady and say something. She shook her head and turned away. He glanced back at me, clearly unable to compute he'd been declined as he mouthed the word *lesbian* to me. Making his way back to our table, he spilled half the beer as he tripped over the Jack Russell.

Richard was rarely sincere, and when he was, one still presumed he was insincere. He'd left a trail of wrecked relationships in his wake and still believed he was the symptom, not the cause. I figured to an extent that was fair, because to share a bed with Dr. Headley was surely to play Russian roulette, with the weapon being any organism fond of warm, damp places.

It turned out today that he was losing his touch. The young woman at the bar gave him a withering look, shook her head pityingly, and turned back to her drink.

"Methinks your technique isn't so impressive in the twenty-first century, Richard," I said with a smirk. "Don't tell me we've found somebody who's able to resist you? And don't forget the age divided by two plus seven rule. She fails that. She's only about eighteen. I have a suggestion, though. How about instead of writing your book, you seek redemption for your carnal sins and perhaps work out why every woman with whom you ever had a relationship left you?"

For a brief moment, I could see that my comment resonated, but he quickly adjusted his thoughts to the constant assertion that the fault lay with the other person. Not in a misogynistic way. Simply in his struggle to imagine a different explanation. Or to see himself as anything other than a prize every woman desired.

Then he proceeded to describe his proposal to me. His attempts to discuss how to write about a perfect murder seemed a little too specific for me: a book about a woman in her thirties who was vacuous and expensive?

"It's more than getting rid of the body, Brian," he insisted. "This has got to look as if no crime's been committed." Then he quickly added, "In the book …"

"We need to find a valid reason for your wife to disappear then. Perhaps moving overseas. Or entering a nunnery." Oddly, he didn't correct me about the proposed victim. "Either that or you stage an accident, preferably when you're a hundred miles away. Maybe loosen a wire on the plug to the food mixer."

"She doesn't cook."

"Okay, how about accidental poisoning?"

And so we continued.

I did feel it was a useful exercise to imagine how one might get away with murder. We were discussing how to clear up a cadaver that had passed through an industrial woodchipper when I spotted the soon-to-be-retired Inspector McAlister. He wandered over to our table, a pint of ale in one hand, a whisky chaser in the other, and asked if he could join us. He was already perching himself on the stool, so we had little choice but to enthusiastically nod our delight at his arrival.

I noticed on the table between us a beer mat Richard and I had carefully divided in half to make ourselves makeshift notepads, since neither of us had brought anything to write on. On my half of the mat, worryingly in my handwriting, were five scenarios:

> Fall from a height.
> Sepsis.
> Poison — mushrooms?
> Exsanguination.
> Blunt trauma — pay someone to assault her?

As nonchalantly as I could, I put my beer on top of the words, then casually dragged the mat toward me. And for today at least that was the end of the proposal, since discussing murder in front of a senior police officer wasn't something generally recommended. Strangely, Richard didn't ask him to contribute to the book's plot.

I hadn't seen McAlister since his fifty-fifth birthday party to which I'd been invited partly, I surmised, out of guilt that he'd all but accused me of the Kilminster murders before the real perpetrator had become clear. I remained certain I'd done most of his work for him, particularly since he had a reputation for watching every sporting event airing on television and conducting his investigations from his sofa.

When I got home, there was the usual mayhem. The children were there with their friends. Both of my kids were doing a sponsored walk to raise money for equipment for the school gym. I wasn't quite sure why the responsibility to pay for essential gym equipment sat with the parents but kept my thoughts to myself.

"How does it work?" I asked Louisa.

"You pay me for every lap of the gym that I walk, Daddy." Louisa always added the word *Daddy* when she wanted something.

"Okay, well how many laps do you think you're going to do?"

"I don't know. Perhaps twenty?"

"Sure, I'll give you 5 pence per lap."

"Shelley's dad is paying 20 pence per lap."

"Oh, right. Well, let's do the same then," I agreed, feeling trapped.

I worked out that this would cost me £4 for each of my two kids, and with an internal grimace, I signed the sponsor forms. Moments later, I was hijacked by two of their friends, both clutching identical forms. In unison, they asked, "Will you sponsor me, too, please?"

This was awkward. It wouldn't look good to decline to sponsor my children's friends. But should I offer them the same amount? I spied Catherine on the other side of the kitchen; her expression answered the question for me. With significant bitterness, I signed off on another £8.

I'd recounted my meeting in the supermarket with Sir Desmond to Richard and McAlister as we'd drunk our beers an hour or so earlier. Headley summarized Leech in one four-letter word, which won't grace the pages of my account. Suffice to say, I told Catherine later that day what Richard had said, edited for her sensibilities.

"Richard called Desmond Leech something pretty bad," I told her.

"Why, what did he say?"

"He called him …" I tried to find the words. "A runt with a *c*."

"A *runc*?"

"Yes, exactly. Pretty disgusting, eh?"

She looked suitably appalled and carried on reading her book. I was relieved not to have had to use the word.

By total coincidence, Sir Desmond's name came up the next day when one of Catherine's friends came around for morning coffee and told us the professor was likely to have a major lawsuit against him after apparently removing the wrong kidney in a patient. The details were currently sparse, but the patient was now on dialysis, since the kidney that had been left in place had cancer and was subsequently removed, also by Leech, the next afternoon.

Perhaps that was why the professor had seemed a little grumpy when I saw him. I felt strangely pleased that karma had caught up with him, though I did briefly spare some sympathy for the victim of the disaster until I heard it was Terry Grimes, one of the sales team at Kilminster Honda who had sold me my current car two years earlier. My colleague, Kathy, had bought the identical vehicle two weeks later for £4,000 less. Grimes's experience with Leech seemed like an appropriate punishment to me, though I didn't share that with Catherine. I figured she'd feel the thought was beneath me. After signing the documents for the Civic and standing up to leave, I recalled that Terry had pointed with his index and middle fingers at me, miming a gun. Then he pulled back on his thumb to cock the "revolver." As he pretended to fire it, he said, "Thank you for letting me share your journeys."

What a load of tosh.

# 5

# PUBLIC TRANSPORT

## SEPTEMBER 10, 2004

I should make it clear that I was culturally and genetically never designed to use public transport. My mother, middle-class but deluded that she was landed gentry, regarded buses with utter horror, as if they were a source of disease. My Civic was terminally ill with an undiagnosable electronics issue and currently sitting on the forecourt of the local Honda dealership, which informed me they were waiting for a part to palliate things prior to its inevitable demise. I wondered if God had ordained this after my uncharitable thoughts about their salesman, Terry Grimes, who still languished in Kilminster Hospital with no kidneys, hoping desperately for some poor family to endure unspeakable tragedy in order to release an organ to him and get him back to work. So, when I found myself in an emergency situation, I finally prepared myself for the second bus journey of my adult life.

The first trip was memorable for the grasp on interpreting statistics shown by two girls discussing the AIDS epidemic back in 1983. They were sitting right behind me on the top of a double-decker in Bristol City Centre.

"They say by 1990, one in four people will have AIDS," said the first.

Her sister replied, "Well, obviously it'll be our Barry, won't it?"

My second public transport mission was to a sewing machine store in Kilminster. I'd moved Catherine's sewing machine off the dining room table, and somehow as I swung it to the floor, caught it on a chair whereupon a metal round thing flew off. It wasn't clear what the part was, but I gathered it would be disproportionately expensive. Believing this could all be rectified before Catherine discovered the breakage, I elected to replace the part and never have to confess. In principle, that was the wise thing to do. For example, if you broke a mug, why admit it? It was far better to balance the mug precariously on a cupboard where it would crash to the countertop when the door was next opened.

Catherine had taken our other car to drive to work, which meant walking five miles or catching a bus. I was intrigued by the prospect but put on some old jeans, since the thought of sitting in a bus seat immediately filled me with thoughts of The Great Unwashed. I wasn't prepared to sully a pair of my brown corduroy Marks & Spencer casuals.

There were four of us at the bus stop: a man in his seventies who was a stranger to showers, sported a dirty white beard, and had an alarmingly orange section of moustache from his sixty-a-day smoking habit; a woman in her late sixties with a tartan pull-along shopping cart whom my mother would say was "the type" for public transport; and a young girl of about eighteen or so with an attitude and pink fluffy earphones. When the 591 bus arrived, I boarded it with a sigh.

Only four seats were available. Shopping-cart woman sat in the disabled access chair near the front, looking around as if to challenge anybody who might tell her she was as able-bodied as everybody else on the bus. That left one empty seat next to a man who by his girth already occupied two, and a pair of empty spots halfway up on the left. The young girl sat next to me, a little too close for comfort. She was listening to something that was probably rap, post–Electric Light Orchestra, and thus beyond my time. We were in town fifteen minutes later. No need to find a parking space, I reflected.

I headed first to Marks & Spencer to use the washroom where I thoroughly scrubbed my hands. When I'd accidently held the metal grab rail as I'd exited the bus, I felt as if my hands had been dipped in the corpse of a plague victim. The washroom had a hand dryer and no paper towels, meaning I had to hang around until somebody else entered so I could escape without reinfecting my hands on the door handle.

The sewing machine shop was down an ancient alley not far from the marketplace and had probably changed little in the past three hundred years. A bell on the door rang as I entered to be greeted by that indefinable smell that all small appliance shops seem to have — machine oil, beeswax polish, and dust. There was a white-haired man of about seventy wearing some sort of grey lab coat with the shop logo over the left breast.

"I've broken our sewing machine," I explained. "I was hoping to fix it before the end of the day."

I reached into my pocket for a scrap of paper on which I'd written the part number I'd found in the manual that came with the machine. Pulling it out, I gave it to the man at the counter along with the round bit of metal.

"What's this?" he asked.

"I thought the model number would be useful."

"I don't think this is what you meant to give me, son." He passed the paper back. "And it looks like you may have more important things to do than replace your bobbin. Anyway, there's nothing wrong with this one."

I took the piece of paper from him and glanced at it. It wasn't the supermarket receipt where I'd written the model number. It was a handwritten note:

> Hi Dad,
> This might be a bit of a shock, but I'm your daughter. You abandoned me twenty years ago. Wanna get to know me?
> We've got some catching up to do. I think we should meet up soon. Call me. Or perhaps I should just pop round and see you. I'm sure your wife would be pleased to meet me!
> Jess
> 09828 928 8229

My legs began to shake uncontrollably, and I broke into a total body sweat. The old man peered at me with a lifetime of experience but said nothing, though perhaps there was an almost imperceptible lifting of one eyebrow. Pushing my way out of the shop into the alley,

I almost tripped over the same dog that had wrapped its leash around me in the pub a few days earlier.

Luckily, I avoided having to use public transport for a second time because a car drew up beside me, and there was my brother, Harvey. He lowered the window and offered to drive me home, which I eagerly accepted. Traditionally a little heavy-footed, he shot into the road, forcing the car behind to swerve, and was already twenty above the speed limit before he reached the edge of town. Going through a red light was the final straw for the car he'd cut off. To my horror, the driver of that vehicle turned on flashing blue lights.

Harvey seemed unperturbed as he pulled over. He reached across me to the glove compartment, I assumed to get his driver's licence and insurance documents.

"You've done it now, Harv," I said. "I reckon you added up at least nine penalty points."

He smiled. "Oh, Brian, you're always such a Negative Nancy. Watch and learn, brother."

Instead of his licence and insurance documents, Harvey retrieved a moss-green plastic bag that he quickly opened while I nervously glanced behind me at the police officer climbing out of the squad car. My brother merely rested the bag on his thighs.

Before I could say another word, I was overcome by the stench of dog excrement so strong that it felt as if I were eating it. Harvey lowered the window and grinned up at the police officer. "Good day, Officer. How can I help you?"

The police officer gawked as if he'd been struck by a wooden mallet. Then he took a step backward, narrowly avoiding being taken out by a passing car. Maintaining his position initially five feet from our vehicle, he hurriedly stepped back farther.

"Sir, I believe you jumped the red light back there while driving at fifty," he began. But then his demeanour crumpled, and he added, "I'm going to let you off with a warning. You need to be more careful."

Rapidly, he went back to his car, taking great gulps of air. Meanwhile, I gagged uncontrollably and wound down my window, which didn't help one bit, so I thrust the door open and staggered out of Harvey's car, sucking in mouthfuls of exhaust fumes from a passing bus — still better than my brother's bag of month-old dog poo he obviously kept in his car for unexpected police stops.

"Still no points on my licence!" shouted Harvey as he knotted up the bag and put it back in the glove compartment.

I didn't tell him about the note in my pocket. When I got home, I hid it in the pages of a book, then retrieved it and rushed to the phone, lifting the receiver and listening to the dial tone. But I didn't go ahead with the call. I replaced the handset in its cradle, still holding the note, and went to find a chair to sit and worry.

# 6

# WHO'S THE DADDY?

## SEPTEMBER 15, 2004

Over the next few days, I decided not to discuss the note from "Jess" with Catherine. For starters, I found it challenging to believe I could have another child, since I hadn't been particularly prolific on the dating front.

There was Laura with the days-of-the-week panties, but she didn't count, since it had never gone beyond me reading *Monday* on her crotch on a Thursday. While not as prolific as Julio Iglesias, I at least had some vague dating success before marrying. I didn't suffer the fate of one of my roommates, Bruce, whose own attempted conquest had been equally unlikely to result in conception. He'd been suffering from a painful lump on his anal margin for a few days and decided that a carefully rolled-up length of toilet paper could act as a pad to mitigate the discomfort.

One evening, he was certain this would be the night he'd lose his virginity, but instead, as he strolled naked to the light switch to achieve the necessary mood lighting, he heard the romantic words "What the ruddy 'eck is that? Looks like you sat on a fuckin' guinea pig."

"Well, it doesn't call for vulgarity" was the most he could respond with, feeling that a detailed account of his perianal issues was unlikely to result in sex. I bought him some cream for the condition to try to lessen his despair but was unable to prevent him from being called "Cottontail" for the next four years.

My only other possibility was a rather clingy girl named Amelia. She insisted on taking me to Blackpool, perhaps the worst place in the United Kingdom — a seaside resort with amusement arcades, donkey rides, candy floss, and people having fun, four of the many things I couldn't abide.

"Oh, look, Brian, there's an old-fashioned gypsy caravan. You can get your palm read."

I argued for a minute or two until she agreed to pay. Upon entering the caravan, I was greeted by a woman who resembled Ronald Reagan a little, though with more hoop earrings and beads.

"First, you must cross my palm with silver," she said.

"Say that again."

"You must cross my palm with silver."

"I literally have no clue what you're talking about."

"You need to give me 50 pence."

Why hadn't she said that in the first place?

She asked me if I currently, previously, or might sometime in the future work in a very large building. I struggled to think of any job in which the answer wouldn't be yes. Perhaps being in the navy.

She gazed at my palm for about five minutes, offering me various predictions of my future.

When I left the caravan, Amelia immediately asked what the woman had told me.

"She says I'll get married and have children."

Amelia blushed and appeared very happy.

"With a woman whose name begins with the letter *C*."

Within about eight seconds, the mood chilled and Amelia folded her arms, which meant trouble. Then she started walking ahead of me a little too fast. Another sign of discontent.

That was the end of the relationship. We drove home in silence, and a further period of relationship famine ensued.

The more I thought about it, the more likely it had to be the girl on the bus who had slipped the note into my pocket. But she was only in her late teens, maybe a little older. Nowadays, though, it was hard to tell. That meant the mother of Jess had to be one of three women. Well, perhaps two. Still, I was unclear why anyone wouldn't have told me I was a father. I chose not to call Jess … yet. I slept fitfully for the next four nights, anxious about how this was going to ever come to a satisfactory conclusion.

Only a few days later, on a rainy early evening when it was already getting dark, I popped down to the local Shell station's small grocery store to get some milk for the following morning. I grabbed a pint of milk and a couple of chocolate bars and was about to pay when I spotted the girl who had sat next to me on the bus, still wearing her fluffy pink earphones. As I'd earlier surmised, she had to be the one who had passed the note to me. I was certain she was watching me from the end of the aisle and assumed she'd followed me here to confront me. Approaching her, I asked her how old she was.

"Fourteen," she replied.

"Oh, I thought you were closer to twenty." Then I clumsily added, "Look, Jessica, I know you want me to be your daddy, but we need to talk about it."

She stared at me in horror, clearly devastated that I was denying paternity. Crying, she ran from the shop, grabbed her bike, and headed off in the direction of my house. I feared she was going to challenge me at home and there was about to be a major showdown, but I didn't see her again that evening. Sleeping little that night again, I woke up at three in the morning, realizing that if Jessica was only fourteen, I couldn't possibly be her father.

Relieved that it was now impossible for her to be my daughter, I stole a couple of hours of sleep before waking at five when I had the awful insight that perhaps it was a different girl who had put the note in my pocket. I shoved this notion into a box in the back of my mind and thought nothing more about it until my friend, Norm Brown, paid the price a few days later.

# 7

# MEDICAL SCHOOL

## SEPTEMBER 1980

I thought my problems had started in the past few years, but actually, on balance, they began when I arrived at medical school, young, innocent, and finely moulded by a private education into an entitled idiot who hadn't quite reached the point of realization that what I didn't know in life amounted to ninety-nine-point-nine percent and what I did know would probably turn out to be wrong in the future.

By the end of the first day of medical school, I was ready to drop out. I'd endured Freshers' Week and the trauma of being removed from home and transplanted to a residence hall with five hundred other people where, it seemed, everybody had made lifelong friends within forty-eight hours. Meanwhile, I reluctantly left my room and went to the residence hall's bar where I sat like a Billy No-Mates before sloping back upstairs to listen to Electric Light Orchestra on my Sony Walkman.

A man of about fifty with a grey ponytail and denim jacket was there. Around him thronged about twenty impressionable female teenagers hanging on to his every word. I assumed he was a tutor, or perhaps the cleaner. But it turned out he was what was known as a mature student doing a degree in Japanese art from the first millennium. Several girls found this very exotic, no doubt attracted by his maturity. I made a decision there and then that older men with ponytails would never feature among my friends and chose not to adore this fellow whom I suspected was a creep. But as a system for recruiting young girls, it seemed that returning to do a degree close to retirement age was working well for him.

The Freshers' Fair was on Tuesday and was an event in which about two hundred different university clubs tried to lure young innocents to join. Every table had overly jolly second- or third-year students befriending naive newbies and persuading them to sign up.

The students in the Christian Union were particularly enthusiastic, full of smiles, acne, and spectacles, but were a little too earnest, asking me if I'd found God yet as they thrust pamphlets into my hand. The Rugby Club had set up its station in the Student Union Bar. They were clearly having a whale of a time squatting from the top of a stepladder and trying to defecate into a pint glass. Not entirely what I'd imagined when I left for university, but they seemed to have recruited the most students. I joined the Kayak and Photography Clubs because I knew my parents would feel reassured that I was settling in. The rest of the week consisted of social events that mainly involved drinking and sex, but not with me.

The end of the week was a relief, and I fervently hoped that once classes commenced I'd find a like-minded individual, a fellow misanthropist without a regional accent who preferred to go hiking rather than to Roxy's Nightclub and perhaps listened to Electric Light Orchestra.

The first lecture of the first day was given by the dean of the medical school, a man who had been born in 1925, had fought in one world war, and had witnessed the birth of Britain's National Health Service. The dean wasn't a man to offend, since he appeared to have no qualms throwing students off the course. He wore half-moon spectacles that he peered over with cold eyes, over which overgrown eyebrows erupted each the size of a hairbrush.

"Look around," he told us. "Out of one hundred and twenty of you in the room today only one hundred will make it through to the end of the year. Of the hundred who pass, on average fifty-five will end up becoming general practitioners." His face indicated this was an undesirable outcome, for he was a professor of surgery. "Twenty will find a medical specialty and fifteen will become surgeons. There will be three psychiatrists, three gynecologists, and two pediatricians. The final two will end up in Public Health." He said this with a sneer to a ripple of laughter at such a dire fate befalling the last two survivors not thrown off the course.

"Public Health," he repeated. "A career looking at head lice in kids and a life praying for someone to get diarrhea at the local Indian restaurant, or the ultimate goal, a pandemic." Five students in the front row burst into sycophantic guffaws. I was soon to learn that they sat in the front row for the next few years. Perhaps it allowed more scope to get their tongues closer to the professor's bum.

"You're professionals. Remember that. Step out of line on this course and you'll be penalized." I had not heard the word *penalized* before. I imagined someone inserting a penis into a liquidizer. That was enough to persuade me to please the dean.

The day continued with each department head — anatomy, biochemistry, physiology, and an odd-looking fellow who seemed inbred and who was responsible for the genetics course — introducing us to the curriculum and requesting us to go out and spend hundreds of pounds on textbooks.

On the second day of medical school, we were familiarized with the dissecting room where twenty humans who had donated their bodies to medical science were slowly peeled apart — six students to a body — over the next twelve months. I'd been a little apprehensive about this, anxious about how I'd respond to my first human cadaver. The overwhelming smell of formalin and the slight chill — they tried to keep the room cool to prevent the corpses from decomposing — added to the atmosphere as one hundred and twenty new medical students approached their dissection tables where human-shaped white sheets covered their "friends" for the next year.

A girl named Jenny fainted and was never seen again. We were already down to one hundred and nineteen students, and for a couple of days we all felt our odds of getting through the first year were a little better, though, in fact, there was a standby group and a new medical student was added to replace her on the third day, who interestingly was imprisoned fifteen years later for persuading elderly widows to add him to their wills.

The rest of the week continued in the same vein: a morning collecting white coats for working on the wards, an afternoon picking up our hospital ID badges, and numerous lectures explaining what professional behaviour was and wasn't.

By the end of the first week, I knew there were seven medical students in our year whose parents were faculty at the medical school. *Thank heavens they got in through merit rather than nepotism*, I thought. Also, in our year we had three Class A drug addicts, two alcoholics, at least six psychopaths, and three students with severe autism who should have become engineers instead.

The class rapidly began to find folk of their type. Rugby players flocked together to discuss drinking beer, Christians discovered one another to consider which churches the heads of departments attended to ensure they were seen there. Students gravitated to others with the same regional accents, and I, Brian Standish, found nobody.

# 8

# ERECTILE DYSFUNCTION

## SEPTEMBER 16, 2004

My Great-Uncle Gerald was a doctor and so were his three sons. He was my maternal grandmother's brother and used to regale us with stories from his career. One told about a patient with a broken leg that Uncle Gerald put into plaster of Paris. Five weeks on, the cast was rattling, and the foot was more painful, so the cast was taken off only to find that that when the initial bandage had been applied, the safety pin had gone right through the middle of the patient's toe. This had subsequently become infected, and being summer, flies had laid eggs in the septic tissue. It was maggots that were rattling. Paradoxically, while the maggots had caused the sound, they'd probably cleared up most of the necrotic skin.

This was a time when doctors were respected and assumed to be right despite the fact that compared to today there was a limited amount they could usefully do. No complaint was forthcoming, and I suspected the patient assumed this was how the fracture was meant to be treated. No Dr. Google existed in those days, and even hairdressers were less expert at medical diagnosis than nowadays.

One of my prized possessions was a gift from Uncle Gerald: a battered brown leather suitcase that when opened contained an almost complete adult skeleton. Well, the bones were all there at least. It took a few hours to reassemble it.

"He was from Bombay," said Gerald. "When I was a medical student, they were the cheapest skeletons you could buy. He was probably around in the nineteenth century and died in the 1920s, ready for me to go to medical school. Maybe he once met the Duke of Wellington. He probably served him a drink." Gerald, like many British men of his generation, lived comfortably in the world of the British Raj and Rudyard Kipling. Clearly, history wasn't his strong point.

This was in the late 1970s, and I'd used the same skeleton through my own training. It now resided in the attic. I genuinely hoped my own children would choose any career but health care, so it would probably remain there. Within a few months, however, the skeleton would be presented as evidence at a murder inquiry.

I already clarified that non-selectively I don't like most people. It's not that I hate most of them; I just don't like them. Perhaps being a misanthropist isn't considered a disorder yet and not against the law, provided one equally dislikes all humans. I was pretty sure my parents had trained me to be like that. A free place at a private school had sealed the deal. And so it is that I enjoy the company of my family and about seven other people. Upon reflection, I like *most* of my family and six other people. And I love dogs.

Among the many people I wouldn't mourn if they perished was our neighbour, Morris Furniss, two doors up — a retired town-hall clerk whose wife had almost certainly wished him dead for the past forty years. I'd never forgiven him for being the instigator of the chain of events that had led to the premature death of my cockerel — a victim of mistaken identity.

I wasn't certain precisely what the Dark Web was, but this man undoubtedly inhabited the blackest corner of it, searching for filth. Something about his oiled back hair and thin moustache made me suspect he was someone who bought rubber gloves, ropes, and industrial lubricants to enact his fantasies. I'd even seen him carrying binoculars, a sure sign of a pervert.

Only a few days earlier, I'd nipped to the washroom in the Green Dragon restaurant where I found Morris putting £1 coins into a wall-mounted vending machine dispensing a pill called "Blue Delight" with the logo "To guarantee her pleasure." It seemed to me that the only way to guarantee his wife's pleasure would be for him to choke on the pill.

Morris was planning to extend his house up to the boundary of our closest neighbour, an eighty-four-year-old widowed woman named Nancy Walton, who was quiet, frail, and weighed about fifty pounds. She had the build of a woman who would undoubtedly fracture several bones if she ever fell.

Everything would have been fine if Morris had accepted that the boundary was three feet closer to his property than he claimed, but his invasion of neighbouring land was the beginning of events that led to my arrest.

Nancy phoned to tell us that the builders had pegged out the boundary of the extension over her property and asked if she should say something. "I'm fairly sure Morris's erection is going to extend over my hedge," she told me.

Obviously, she had the same suspicions I'd voiced over the years. I suggested she call the town-planning department and a lawyer, of course, which Nancy declined to do, since she didn't have the money and didn't wish to offend Morris. She added that Morris had worked in the planning department for the past ten years of his career, so he surely must be correct. Then she started to cry and told me that perhaps she should just say nothing to keep neighbourly relations amicable.

I was furious, but being cut from cowardly cloth, I vented my fury in the kitchen while chopping a carrot, knowing full well I wouldn't likely confront him, either. My brother, Harvey, was having supper with us, so I decided to ask him. He would know how to approach this situation. Harvey knew people. After he told me what to do, I asked, "Do you like your carrots al dente?"

"I went to school with a boy called Allen Dente," he replied.

"Really?"

Harvey stared at me with pity.

Catherine sighed. "You haven't forgotten your vasectomy tomorrow, have you?"

Harvey smirked. "The cruellest cut. Hope he doesn't slice off your bollock."

# 9

# Further Erectile Dysfunction

## September 16, 2004

The logic of getting a vasectomy was irrefutable, since to argue against it seemed to bode poorly. Catherine had borne children, consumed more than her fair share of hormones for five years, and we had reached a point when I should take some responsibility for family planning. How could I disagree? More specifically, I was to lie on an operating table while a colleague spent fifteen minutes with a scalpel next to my nuts.

And the day had now arrived. I was booked first on the list and was lying under a bright light, steadfastly looking upward while my genitals were displayed and surrounded by a green cloth for more artistic presentation. At this point, Mary Taylor, not my surgeon, who had an endoscopy patient in the adjacent operating room, walked into chat to Dominic Spencer, who was performing my vasectomy. They started to discuss the challenge of finding dressings while Mary held her gaze on the display in front of her, occasionally glancing up and grinning at me, then returning her stare to my nuts. Mary was a fearsome woman — four inches taller than I was with a cold calmness that caused most males intense anxiety from twenty feet away. The fact that I still suspected her of colonoscoping her colleague to death added to the literal naked fear that riffled through me.

She shot me one more derisory smirk and left the room, leaving me to listen to Dominic's bedside manner. He listed a range of adverse outcomes, including infection and reaction to the local anesthetic.

"Sometimes we cut the artery to the testis in error instead of the vas," he started. "It's a little inconvenient because your testis will go black and drop off, but from a practical perspective the outcome is the same."

I sensed my testes retracting to somewhere around my kidneys as he offered his words of comfort.

"You may feel a little pinch now," he murmured as somewhere down the table somebody attached a giant battery jump cable to my scrotum.

Twenty minutes later, I left considerably less tender than I'd be in a few hours, and things were pretty good for at least the next six days, at which point Catherine was out of the house and I took a tentative peek, owing to a little more discomfort than I'd expected. To my horror, there were globules of pus around each suture, as well as a large angry red swelling along the scar, so much that the stitches looked as if they'd cut through the scrotum like cheese wire. I figured the wound might have already knitted together and that the wisest plan was to remove a couple of the stitches. And, of course, I'd do the procedure myself, which was why a few moments later I was sitting cross-legged on the kitchen floor wielding a large pair of scissors from the kitchen drawer, since I couldn't find a smaller pair in the house.

With some delicate finesse, I removed the first suture, breathed a sigh of relief, then tackled the next one, which proved harder because I couldn't get the blade of the giant scissors under the stitch. In the end, though, I managed, whereupon the wound immediately gaped open for nearly an inch of its length. Seized with panic, I imagined one or both testes dropping out and rolling across the kitchen floor, so I scootched across the floor to our junk drawer, opened it from a sitting position, and reached up with my left arm to feel around for some tape. When I found what I needed — some red electrical tape — I proceeded to hold the edges of the wound together as best I could.

I was unable to face the ignominy of a trip to the hospital for a proper assessment, but the fates were kind to me, and over the next few days, despite my attempts at sabotage, everything healed up. On the day I pulled off the electrical tape, Catherine began to have further maternal musings about having one more child. But that ship had definitely sailed.

# 10

# MISTAKEN IDENTITY

## OCTOBER 2, 2004

I remember the start of the day very well. I'd eaten a strawberry yoghurt that tasted disgusting. Definitely off, despite the sell-by date being three weeks hence. Ian Beaney, Catherine's brother, had asked us, quite oddly, to look after eight yoghurts for him, but when he didn't return for them after two weeks, I ate the first and threw the rest away. Of course, by total coincidence about an hour later, Ian arrived to collect them. He became very flustered and burrowed through our kitchen trash to collect the unused yoghurts. I suspected he was up to his usual scurrilous behaviour but was unable to work out what a few yoghurts could be used for. In a few weeks, I understood a little more.

Richard Headley and I were meeting at the White Horse on Kilminster High Street for a game of cribbage. I had no idea what inspired him to call me to make this suggestion, but this was our second pub visit in two weeks, and we were in grave danger of becoming proper friends.

Dr. Headley, charmer and rake, was sitting there in his usual weekday attire of blue gingham shirt, a pointless silk scarf dangling around his neck. In addition, he sported an alarming pair of brick-red trousers and brown tassel loafers with no socks. I wondered what he wanted from me. He wouldn't choose to spend time with me unless there was something in it for him. Richard was so good at lying that he began to believe his own lies and step into the role. The ultimate in method acting.

"What drugs would a pathologist routinely check for in an unexpected death?" he asked me, as if that was the most natural question. "And if, say, you accidentally made a soup with hemlock in it, how fast would you die?"

"Well, that beats saying hello," I replied. "But sorry, Richard, I have no idea how fast you'd die. I remember my uncle's cow died in six hours. And in terms of screening, it depends on the imagination of the pathologist. If you died in Kilminster, then for sure the pathologist would call it pneumonia. He likes the simple life as you know. Is this for your book?"

"Yes, of course. What else would it be?" He kicked a bag from the supermarket containing various vegetables farther under the table.

Richard had his own cribbage pegboard engraved with his name and family crest. He also had his playing cards made with the same crest. We dealt six cards each, and I was about to discard a pair into the crib when I spotted Milky Norm at the bar.

When we were young, there were television commercials for a white chocolate bar called a Milky Bar. They featured, over the years, a series of short-sighted blond boys wearing a Stetson and round glasses playing the part of the Milky Bar Kid. Milky claimed to have been the Milky Bar Kid in the 1980s, and every so often he'd call out the catchphrase known to a generation: "The Milky Bars are on me!" He even still dyed his hair blond and wore a little pair of round glasses to complete the look. Norm wore cowboy shirts with little black laces as ties and ridiculous pointed boots with Cuban heels.

A brief research effort revealed that this was a total fabrication on his part, but he had lived the character for so long that everybody accepted it. It was fun to see his face when hoping for guffaws of laughter, though more often than not he received confused stares when he told people that "the Milky Bars are on me."

Milky worked for a window company and had recently installed the windows in our house during the renovation that followed a gas explosion in our kitchen. I put him at about thirty-five years old, but he lived the role of eternal teenager. In former days, people probably would have called him the village idiot, but nowadays that term wasn't allowed, so I referred to him as a "hamlet dweller" with an element of intellectual modesty.

Just then, a man with a shaved skull and wearing a Manchester United football shirt walked into the White Horse and approached Milky. He was about five foot four but stocky and powerful-looking, like a pit bull terrier. I recognized the man vaguely. In fact, I believed he lived a short way up the road from me. Interestingly, he had the names of his two children tattooed on his right forearm. One imagined him having to check every so often lest he forgot their names. Now he singled out Milky and demanded, "Are you …?"

Milky smiled. "Guilty, as charged. The Milky Bars are —" Unfortunately, he didn't manage to complete his well-worn phrase.

The man grabbed Milky by the throat. "You leave my daughter alone, you disgusting pervert."

He threw Milky to the floor, then snatched his beer and poured it over Norm's face. Except it wasn't his beer. It belonged to the man sitting on a bar stool next to where Norm had been standing to order a drink, who now joined the fray as if he'd been waiting for this opportunity for years. The owner of the pint climbed down from his stool and grabbed Manchester by the football shirt before manhandling him out of the White Horse. Milky was clearly a little confused and shaken.

Richard had put down his cards, and with an excited grin, jumped up from his chair to get a better view of what was happening outside. Those who didn't leave stared at Milky, who realized he was in danger of being remembered for chasing after teenagers and not for advertising white chocolate.

I followed Richard outside where Manchester was using his lexicon of vulgarity while a girl whom I assumed was his daughter stood to one side, pale and frightened. She had a pair of fluffy pink earphones around her neck, caught my eye, and raised a finger to point at me, trying to get through to her father who was still screaming obscenities. Before Manchester cottoned on to what was happening, there was the blessed sound of two police sirens a hundred yards away.

When I ducked back into the pub, everything was now alarmingly clear to me. Milky was bravely sitting up at the bar again, pale and tremulous, claiming mistaken identity. Of course, he was totally correct, but I felt perhaps now wasn't the time to clarify the situation. Richard joined me a couple of minutes later, telling me that Manchester was on his way to Kilminster Police Station. I didn't have the urge to play cribbage anymore and beckoned Norm over to our table.

Milky lived in a small bedsit above the Silver Cod fish-and-chip shop where his mother, who was christened Deborah but had changed her name to Saffron, had worked before becoming a full-time doula. She had even tried to change Norm's name to Moonbeam. Saffron's career had lately faltered after our friend, Tracey, had failed to take advice on natural approaches to childbirth and had gone full epidural during her first labour. As a result, many of Saffron's mothers-to-be were beginning to doubt the claims that a pre-birth diet of tofu and almond milk would lead to an analgesic-free birth.

Behind the Silver Cod was a small yard containing a half-deflated birthing pool and a discarded box of whale music cassettes. Saffron had recently discovered her real talent: she could communicate with *the other side.*

Milky turned to Headley. "You know, it's funny that I've seen you tonight. Mum was talking about Kilminster Hospital just before I left. She says one of the consultants died of a heart attack, but she had an image come to her from *the other side* of a black snake let loose by a woman."

Richard gave me a meaningful look. It was an open secret in Kilminster that Colin Marks hadn't died of a heart attack but had met his death a few moments after apparently performing his own colonoscopy. Was the colonoscope the black snake? There had been a suspicion that a third party had been involved in his demise, but that was never pursued because there were a number of important sporting events on the TV at the time and they were the primary focus of Inspector McAlister. Norm's mother wouldn't have to go far in Kilminster to hear the gossip, most of it started by Dr. Headley himself at the Kilminster squash club.

"Did the black snake crawl up his arse?" asked Richard.

Milky looked a little confused. "I think it just bit him. I never asked. I'll check with Mum."

Once again, Headley's attempts to corner me had been thwarted. By seven o'clock, we were ready to leave.

During most summers in Kilminster, a few families of travellers parked in a field on the north side of town. This invariably led to several weeks of anxious correspondence in our local newspaper, usually about crime rates, but every year they moved on. The travellers generally left a confusing number of broken washing machines and prams behind, and I never quite worked out where all the debris came from.

As I left the White Horse, I saw one of the travellers standing outside a bakery. She was holding a basket full of heather bunches and appeared to be about ninety-five years old but was probably forty. The woman held one out toward me, asking me if I wished to buy some lucky heather. I suspected that it wasn't, in fact, lucky, so I deviated by a couple of yards to get past her at which point she thrust a bony finger at me and yelled, "A curse on you, Brian!"

How had she known my name? I froze inside and scurried back to my car, which had finally been fixed, feeling sure something terrible was about to happen to me. As I climbed into the car, I noticed my hospital ID tag pinned to my jacket and smiled to myself, relieved, though still shaken. I pulled out of the space and drove straight into a bus.

# 11

# Delivering Babies

## April 1982

"Draw your knees up toward your bottom and then just let your legs fall apart," I said, having heard the consultant use the same sentence.

"Can you see my chuff now?" was the reply from the other end of the table. This was a northern lass, who from where I sat was a stranger to the bathroom but a well-recognized sight in her local fish-and-chip shop. Such was her efficiency in storing spare calories that there was very little room to work with, and this was my first attempt at inserting a speculum.

"That ruddy 'urt," she said, reassuring me further. Try as I might, I never did get to see her cervix, though I turned to the consultant eagerly watching me and told him I had a perfect view.

I continued this deceit for the next nine attempts on other unsuspecting patients and ticked off a little box in the logbook we were required to complete to record our procedural competence. One thing that was definite was that whatever specialty I chose it wouldn't involve a vagina. I was apparently immune from appreciating the gift of nature and was clear in my mind that I would pursue no specialty involving moistness, sputum, or other bodily waste.

By then, I was halfway through my obstetrics-and-gynecology block and couldn't wait for it to end. Indeed, had an offer come up, instead of attending clinics, for me to eat raw offal for the next fortnight — which did, of course, bear some similarities to the specialty — I'd have seized the chance.

I was also required to deliver ten babies. The first one I remembered very well because it just sort of flopped out after a vague push from the mother, who uttered the memorable lines, "I'm dying for a ciggy. Let's get this over with."

The second baby also emerged efficiently. The father gazed at me is if I were some sort of superhero. The truth was it was about as amazing as watching somebody defecate in terms of timing and difficulty. Nonetheless, he turned to me and asked, "What's your name?"

I was hugely flattered because they were going to name the baby after the hero who had delivered it — meaning I stood at the foot of the bed while Mother Nature took over. "Brian," I replied.

Try as he might, the father was unable to hide the disappointment from in eyes. Needless to say, the baby ended up with an equally terrible name, Reginald. Who, in the latter half of the twentieth century would ever think of that name for a baby? Interestingly, there was a young man with the name Reginald eighteen years later convicted of armed robbery. I wonder if I had the honour of delivering him, and if his destiny was already set in stone at that moment. Was he genetically primed for crime?

I didn't have much recollection of the next three babies other than a constant feeling that the midwives found all medical students somewhat irritating and had their hands hovering around the vulva the whole time, gradually leaning into me and pushing me away. My incompetence, I fear, was very apparent to them. I only delivered one more, though once again I did manage to get my experience ticked off as if I'd done ten.

With my final baby, I rather lost heart because I'd been into town and bought myself a new pair of Hush Puppies. While the mother was bearing down, the midwife produced a crochet hook from somewhere. I'd seen her knitting in the staff room and did wonder whether this had come out of her own bag. At the critical moment, I must have averted my eyes, because the next thing I knew about nine gallons of foul-smelling amniotic fluid gushed down over the end of the table like Niagara Falls, soaking the bottom half of my scrubs and seeping into my socks and new shoes.

As it turned out, Hush Puppies suede was the perfect absorptive material for amniotic fluid, which had a unique smell. You could probably say that for most body fluids. None of these "natural" smells would ever find themselves used to scent candles. That evening, I threw the shoes away.

# 12

# Other Scents and a Dinner Party

## October 8, 2004

There were three other smells that always took me to places I'd rather delete from my memory. The first was sawdust on vomit. I had no clear understanding why children threw up all over my primary school classrooms and playground. Perhaps it was the free sour milk we were forced to drink at playtime. Whatever it was, every day there was always a child who puked and someone employed as the sawdust thrower who materialized within seconds of the sick hitting the floor to cover it. In those days, there were auditions on throwing style to achieve the best even spread of sawdust over the pool of vomit.

The next smell was a strangely blended one of toothpaste, feces, deodorant, and sweaty human found in the washrooms of most campsites. Oddly, it was the minty background to the other feral odours that particularly turned my stomach. I could bring this aroma to mind very rapidly, usually when I saw a family heading off for a camping trip.

The third was the whiff of a dog's anal gland, or should I say the taste. Catherine, noting that our spaniel scooched across our new living room rug, insisted I urgently empty his anal glands, a procedure for which I'd had no training. I called Ian, her veterinarian brother, who during this very procedure had temporarily lost his licence to practise. Ian gave me very clear, concise instructions on where the glands were located and how to massage them to relieve the dog. He failed in only one instruction, which was to tell me to keep my mouth closed lest a jet of anal juice eject in an unexpected direction.

And so it was that I found myself early on a Friday evening cleaning my teeth and using copious mouthwash while searching the bathroom drawer for any old antibiotics in case I'd swallowed any of the oily fishy fluid. When I heard the doorbell ring, I remembered a fourth smell.

Catherine had invited Philip and Mavis Perry for supper. We were having three couples to dinner that night, all of whom "we owed," the plan being to pay our social debt in one evening. Philip and Mavis had been previous neighbours, and we kept in touch, seeing them two or three times a year. Philip was about seventy-eight, a little deaf, and inflexible to the point of grumpiness. At some point, a rat had died in his mouth.

A number of negative traits were exhibited by Philip, and as far as I could tell, few positives to balance them out. His catchphrase should have been "Have you got a plunger?" because mysteriously he felt the need to defecate whenever he visited a friend's house. And never had he completed this in fewer than twenty minutes.

Catherine had already let them in, and I took the bottle of home-brewed gooseberry wine from Philip; he'd already opened my fridge and found a bottle of Sauvignon Blanc I was saving for Catherine's birthday. With all the grace I could muster, I took it from him and reached for my corkscrew while Philip, of course, elected to disappear to discharge a cruise ship load of waste.

I'd fitted an automatic fan in the bathroom and hoped that by choosing an industrial model we'd be spared the toxicity we knew was surely heading our way. Fifteen minutes later, after we heard the toilet flush for the third time, Philip emerged, buckling his belt as he returned to our kitchen and dried his wet hands on our tea towel. His fly was still open, revealing a glimpse of urine-stained white underwear.

Remembering our manners, Catherine and I settled into the usual conversations about Philip's wastrel son, who in his eyes could do no wrong. The doorbell rang again, and I experienced a sense of all-too-short relief as I went to let in the other two couples who had arrived in one car. These included my brother, Harvey, with his partner, Dennis Greanleaf, and a work colleague of my own, Mary Taylor, with her new boyfriend, Edward, who was a chain-smoking painter and decorator and who didn't appear to me to share a single attribute with her first husband, a barrister from Bristol. In the history of potentially dreadful dinner parties, it wasn't hard to imagine this current evening winning first prize. I was unable to think of a topic to kick things off.

Harvey lived in Kilminster alone. He lurched from failed relationship to failed relationship. His current partner would be no exception, not for any other reason than the fact that my brother was a relationship butterfly, dancing from one person to the next but never truly committing himself at an emotional level. Dennis was a pharmaceutical representative who occasionally visited me at work to try to persuade me to prescribe Nothrombo.

Mary, meanwhile, was clearly perceived differently by Catherine and me. I found her severe and humourless and had avoided her for several years at work. She reminded me of a surgeon who taught us at medical school.

This surgeon would have on the table in front of him a pile of three volumes of medical notes for a single patient, totalling six inches in height. Turning to us, he'd ask, "When you see a pile of notes this high, what does it tell you?"

Wading through the information in the notes, I tried to summarize what had happened to the unfortunate patient.

"Stop!" he said. "You don't have to read them. If the height of the notes is more than four inches, it means they're nuts." I felt this might be a little unfair, but not content to stop there, he continued. "Have you heard of ECT?"

"No," I admitted.

He grinned. "Electro-convulsive therapy. That's what she needs. Preferably the entire output of the National Grid."

I was shocked, but the power dynamic applied here, so I said nothing. With hindsight, he might have been one of the more compassionate doctors I met during my training. Mary would have fitted in well there.

Meanwhile, Catherine knew Mary through an equally tedious mutual friend and every so often the three would go to the Kilminster Manor Spa to pay an obscene amount of money to have somebody cut their nails for them, after which they would lie around the pool area drinking Prosecco.

Mary's first husband had left her a few months after the death of Colin Marks, who coincidentally had been the subject of our chat with the Milky Bar Kid only a few days earlier. I hoped and prayed that this subject wouldn't be raised this evening just as Catherine said, "Mary, Brian met the most interesting man the other day who claims his mother can communicate with the dead. And you'll never guess who she's been speaking to!"

"I'm sure nobody wants to talk about Colin Marks," I blurted out, leaving the guessing unnecessary. "Milky talks a lot of nonsense, and his mother's just as bad."

Harvey added, "They said he died of a heart attack after shoving a colonoscope up his —"

"Not tonight, Harvey," said Catherine, knowing where many of Harvey's colonically directed conversations could go and recognizing that Philip and Mavis might prefer to talk about the Chelsea Flower Show.

*A woman and a black snake*, I mused as I watched Mary doing a poor job of appearing neutral. I'd long held the suspicion that the death of Colin Marks had been at Mary's hands. Perhaps the Milky Bar Kid's mother really could communicate with *the other side.*

Catherine's food saved the evening, and somehow, we managed to reach ten o'clock when Philip and Mavis decided to leave because they had a Rotary Club Bring and Buy Sale the following day. Mary had drunk the best part of a bottle of gooseberry wine and had opened up considerably, losing the resting-bitch face and garrulously describing how she'd met her painter and decorator, who went by Eddie, and at one point telling Catherine how to have sex on a stepladder. Even Eddie realized this might have breached the Dinner

Party Code, though I suspect he was secretly proud that we now knew why there was a duck-egg blue stain on their living room carpet. Eddie then mentioned he'd been asked to paint the planned extension two doors up.

"What do you make of Morris Furniss?" I asked.

"Complete twat, but one with money," replied Eddie, giving me a hint how a contractor viewed his clients. I wondered what he said about us, since he was currently wall-papering our stairwell with a hideously expensive paper that Catherine had chosen, which looked like one of those optical illusions where the squares seemed as if they were going to move. I'd agreed to the design, mainly to get out of the shop faster, but I now seriously wondered if it might be the cause of a fatal fall down the stairs.

The conversation moved to our immediate neighbour, Nancy, and her anxiety that Morris's plans involved building on her own property. Mary mentioned a case her ex-husband had defended in which construction had ended abruptly when a Viking bracelet was discovered as the foundations were being dug. In the absence of any ancient relics for Morris to bury in his potato patch, we felt this might be a vain hope, though in the darkest recesses of my mind I had a thought that I failed to hold on to. A few moments later, it was gone, though I knew at some point it would reappear, probably in the middle of the night. Viking remains were exactly what Nancy needed.

As the evening came to a close, I recalled the stepladder was in our garage and decided I had no plans to explore how he and Mary had found their carnal pleasures. We washed the dishes before going to bed, and I noted that Catherine was drying with the tea towel Philip had used and which I'd intended to burn.

# 13

# SHE DIDN'T PREDICT IT

## OCTOBER 16, 2004

Just to the left of the glass door of the Silver Cod fish-and-chip shop was another wooden one painted red, likely as long ago as the early 1970s. The paint was now peeling off and had faded to a dull pink. The average passerby might miss the small piece of cardboard with the words CLAIRVOYANT. GO UPSTARES written in black marker pen, the spelling mistake not noticed.

I'd been there a few times, usually to bring Milky home from the pub. When you pushed open the door, you always involuntarily caught your breath as the smell of inadequately emptied cat litter boxes mixed with fried cod hit your nostrils.

To remain keen to communicate with a lost loved one or to ask the medium whether to accept the new job at Terry's Newsagent or not, those visiting the clairvoyant were advised to take a final breath of fresh air from outside and attempt to breath slowly before climbing the stairs while noticing the worn Axminster carpet.

At the top of the stairs, in the same handwriting, was a similar notice asking customers to take a seat. There were two plastic chairs on the upstairs landing suspiciously similar to those in the Silver Cod next door. The chairs were placed on either side of an aquarium that might or might not have once contained fish. The glass was so thick with algae that nothing could be seen.

Neither Milky nor I were present on the day an unknown visitor took this route but didn't take a seat, instead stealthily pushing open the door that led to the inner sanctum, a bedroom converted into the spiritual communication temple. Fairy lights framed the curtained window, and a patchouli oil burner filled the room with essence, the better to summon lost spirits, no doubt.

I imagined there would have been an odd sound, probably the noise a skull made if a crystal ball were smashed over the temple, shortly followed by a muffled thud as the body hit the floor. Then likely a toilet flushed and there were returning footsteps, and finally, the echo of the mystery visitor hurriedly rushing downstairs, out of the building, and into the street. The final sound would have been an *oomph!* — Harvey exhaling as the visitor ran into him, causing him to drop his battered sausage and chips.

About two hours later, the clairvoyant's son, Norman, sometimes called Moonbeam but mainly referred to as Milky, returned from work. He still hadn't gotten over being assaulted in the pub a few days before and wasn't his normal self.

Milky had never been thumped before. His glasses were bent, and his light blue cowboy shirt was torn around the third buttonhole. He felt desolate and had been on the edge of tears since the incident had happened and hadn't even uttered his six-word catchphrase since the attack.

Norman pushed open the pink door and trudged upstairs, dodging Sooty, his cat. At the top, he paused at the aquarium and reached for a small tube containing fish food from which he took a pinch. Just a spot, because he knew what happened when fish were overfed. His mother had read to him as a child about that. He heard a soft sobbing and walked into the room she worked from, knocking lightly. Norman was fairly certain she didn't have clients this evening. When she didn't respond, he pushed gently. As the door swung open, his eyes adjusted to the fairy lights and he sniffed the smell of the cheap scented candle. His mother was kneeling on the floor, holding her crystal ball with hands covered in blood, slowly rocking over her client, who lay there inert.

"She's dead," moaned his mother with a shuddering sob.

Milky turned on the main lamp. He could see the client was, indeed, dead. Vaguely, he recognized her but couldn't recall from where. However, he knew his mother was a gentle soul, and for her to kill this woman, she must have had a good reason. Gently, he took his mother's hand and led her to the kitchen, then returned to the corpse and dragged it to the middle of the rug, noting the crystal ball was covered in a smear of blood and hair. Next, he went to the kitchen and grabbed a pair of yellow rubber gloves, returned to the glass ball, and carried it to the dishwasher.

Norman was remarkably calm. His mother had murdered a client. Now he needed to dispose of the corpse, which was outside his immediate skill set that was limited to battering cod and driving for the window company.

He only had one friend discreet enough to advise him on what to do at this point, somebody who seemed to have contacts with all strata of society. Milky called my brother, Harvey.

# 14

# Ancient Remains

## October 20, 2004

Morris's extension was well underway. The footings had been dug and the concrete would be poured in the next few days. Part of the adjoining hedge had already been removed, with the footings extended well over the boundary.

In the absence of Viking bracelets, Harvey had had the brilliant idea to leave something else in the foundations to delay the building until our elderly neighbour, Nancy, had found someone to define the property boundary. In fact, I was fairly sure that my plan would put Morris's building work on the town-planning department's radar, compelling him to become a little more reasonable. Morris and Maggy were away this week on one of their many cruises, this time touring the Adriatic for a week. The intention was that the building work would continue while they were away, with the footings to be poured by the end of the week.

I'd bought a balaclava two weeks earlier at an army surplus store in Scarborough while visiting my Auntie Jean, who had recently moved to a new retirement home. She'd been thrown out of the last two, the first time for smoking weed, the second for stealing teaspoons. The cleaner had found thirty-two in her wardrobe. She was also under investigation, having been identified as the probable index case in the home for an outbreak of syphilis. The Scarbrough Syphilis Scandal had hit the *Yorkshire Post* headlines for three consecutive days.

At our local do-it-yourself store, I purchased a head light. In addition, I had a garden trowel. I was planning to wear size ten boots, which I'd borrowed from Harvey. Two sizes too big for me, the better to fool the police. D-day was Thursday because Catherine was going to be out until eleven and it would be dark by seven.

I only had to cross one property, Nancy's, to reach Morris's house but worried that I'd leave a footprint or a piece of cloth on a nail. Both of our properties bordered fields to the south. Therefore, my plan was to climb over our back fence, walk through the field, and enter the Furniss property from there. He had a six-foot fence, so I'd take Eddie's aluminium stepladder, though that would make the trip a little cumbersome. I'd allow myself two hours for the mission, telling the kids I was merely popping up the road. Not a lie, actually. They'd be so engrossed in their homework they'd barely take notice of me.

So, on Thursday, when I got outside, I stepped to the back garden and headed to the end where I'd already left the ladder. I took with me the garden trowel and the brown leather suitcase containing the skeleton of the unknown East Indian. When I was near the top of the ladder ready to perch on top of my fence, I heard a rustling of leaves followed by the ferocious barking of my own dog. I tried to get him to stop, but he just got worse. I put my hand in something wet, cold, and slightly tacky on the ladder. In a flash, I remembered the stepladder gymnastics of Mary and Eddie, recoiled in horror, and the stepladder overbalanced.

Winded and discouraged, I lay in our raspberry bush still clutching the suitcase. A light flashed on in the living room, and one of the kids stared down at the garden where our dog was greeting me as if I'd been away for a year. The task at hand would have to be postponed for an hour.

I had to wait ten more minutes in the garden for the children to return to their rooms before slinking back into the house. The mission needed to be completed, but this time I abandoned the garden route and simply strolled up the road, meeting nobody. No cars passed me as I made my way the two hundred feet to Morris's home and slipped through the garden gate at the side of the house.

The footings were almost complete and ready for the concrete to be poured. It was the work of about twenty minutes to scrape a few more inches of soil from the bottom of the ditch and place the skeleton in his final resting place. I did as good a job as I could to make sure the bones were reasonably anatomically placed, including ribs and vertebrae. Then I sprinkled soil over everything, figuring a large digger would scrape the bones up in the morning and I wouldn't have to be overly concerned about accuracy. Then I returned to the skull and dusted off some of the soil I'd covered it with, not wanting this corpse to be missed when the concrete was poured.

As I stealthily returned to my own driveway, pulling off the balaclava, a white van came into view. It slowed down, and I realized with dismay that I'd been caught. This was the police. My mouth went dry. Hurriedly, I pulled the balaclava back onto my face and ran down the side path of my house, letting myself in. I ripped off the balaclava, stuffed it into a plastic bag, and raced upstairs where I pulled down the loft ladder and hastily threw the bag into the far corner of the attic, then pushed the ladder back up and closed the hatch.

An emergency wash of my now-filthy clothes was called for. For efficiency, I added a few things from our laundry bin, expecting I'd probably get some valuable points for doing the washing.

By now, I'd expected a banging on the door, or an armed squad to storm up the stairs. But there was silence and then the questioning voice of my daughter. "Why are you only wearing your underpants, Daddy?"

"I'm about to have a shower."

"Why were you in the attic?"

"I thought I heard a mouse."

She accepted the explanation without question or concern and returned to her bedroom. I peeked outside through the window. Nobody was there. The white van had moved up the road and was outside Morris Furniss's house. I decided to take the dog for a walk and get a little closer, so I quickly threw on some old clothes and grabbed the dog leash from its hook by the back door.

I never whistled, but tonight I unexpectedly did so as I set off up the road to ensure that all around knew I was an innocent man simply walking his dog. Slowing down as I reached Morris's driveway, I glanced to my left. There was someone by the footings next to a dark mound, which they then pushed into the hole. The person next started trying to find scoops of earth with his cupped hands to cover whatever had been rolled into the trench. Finally, he grabbed a plank and placed it over the mound before swiftly heading back in my direction. I walked on, whistling, my heart beating fast as I tried to compute what I'd just witnessed.

Ten minutes later, and with Catherine still not due back for another hour, I transferred the washing to the dryer and settled down to watch a documentary. The children came down to kiss me good night.

The following morning, as I was leaving for work, Catherine mentioned that she needed to do some washing and I proudly told her, "No need, darling. I did it last night."

She seemed suitably impressed, and I believed for the next minute her love for me had doubled, until she went to empty the dryer where her new baby-blue cashmere sweater was found, shrunken to a third of its size.

I beat a hasty exit to the car and headed for work, cursing my misfortune. As I was backing out of the driveway, Catherine rushed out to remind me she was going away to her sister's home for a night and asked, "Is my case in the attic?"

I confirmed this, only to remember halfway to work that there was also a bag containing the balaclava I'd worn the previous evening.

# 15

# PROSTATES AND APEX BEATS

## JUNE 1983

The body sat in a bath of dark brown liquid, eyes staring blankly ahead. The left was a glass eye, which looked down and to the side. The right eye had a hazy, almost white cornea. At first glance, it looked as if the man had been severely burnt, most of the skin red and inflamed.

"Good morning," I greeted. "Are you Mr. Baker?"

He grunted and awoke from his snooze. Baker had severe psoriasis. The dermatology ward had six tar baths, and Baker had been admitted for two weeks of treatment for his skin and arthritis. I was a medical student and had been sent to take a full history and perform a physical examination. The latter was impossible, since he'd just been placed in the tar bath. The former wasn't feasible because he was a grumpy bastard who was in no mood to spend half an hour with an upstart medical student.

I was equally unenthusiastic about talking to a naked man in a tar bath. He'd lost vision in both eyes as an army barber when he'd accidentally cut into a scalp abscess that burst into his eyes. After he swore at me for asking to speak to him, he demanded I find a towel and help him out of the bath.

I leave it to the reader to decide whether (a) I happily obliged, helped him out of the bath, assisted him to the shower, and then gently applied cream to his psoriasis in a tender, circular motion, or (b) took advantage of his blindness by silently leaving the therapy room and hotfooting it off the ward to search for the next patient on the list. I wondered to myself if Baker was always going to be an unlikable grump, or whether the cruel hand life had dealt him had turned him from a happy soul to the current curmudgeon. I believed in the well-known aphorism "once a twat always a twat." In other words, had he always been unpleasant?

The next patient was a man of twenty with severe congenital limb deformities and cardiac disease caused by his mother being given thalidomide when she was pregnant. My task as a medical student was to take a history and examine him. He was delightful, and his patience stood in stark contrast to the previous patient. I suspected he'd been doing this weekly for many years and had repeated the same history to hundreds of medical students. This sort of pharmaceutical disaster could never happen again. Who would have imagined that the story of fraud, burying data, kickbacks, and bribery would continue for another generation? Well, all of us, as it turned out.

I wrote up the case ready to give to Professor Philip SanAntonio. My fellow medical students and I were to find the professor and present our cases. I remembered that he didn't turn up to the teaching session because he was away on a pharma-sponsored trip on the Orient Express.

Not altogether disappointed, I was reminded of the men who hung around in the lingerie department in Marks & Spencer, which was only allowed if you were married, holding at least two shopping bags, and glancing up at an interesting mark on the ceiling.

Thinking back, this was when I wrote the first page of my never-completed novel *Meat*. Searching through my old medical school notes recently, just prior to burning them all to prematurely celebrate the end of my medical career, the paper on which I wrote the history was still there.

The first line of *Meat* was: "Charley Steel was sweating. He had worked out how to complete the perfect murder. He fingered his gun nervously." Reflecting on this now, I realized that even in my early twenties the seeds of my misanthropy were already sprouting. I wasn't sure the word *fingered* belonged in any book I wrote and vowed that henceforth I'd never type the word again. Also consigned to the flames were my clinical skills notes.

We were all excited to be taught clinical skills — the opportunity to see real patients after endless weeks of anatomy and physiology lectures. The ancient art of the physical exam almost had mystical status.

Split into twenty groups of five students, our groups were sent each week to different specialists so that, for example, one would learn the examination of the shoulder, another the examination of the heart. Over the next twelve weeks, we rotated through the various parts of the body, and by the end of three months became relatively familiar with how to examine patients.

The first ten students sent to learn the prostate exam had a rough start. Dr. Philip SanAntonio, lingerie loiterer, for reasons unexplained, volunteered to be a live patient. Eagerly, he took off his trousers and underwear and jumped onto the examination table, hanging his bottom over the side. He had the modesty to drape a small green towel over his buttocks to preserve dignity. Handing over a full tube of lubricating jelly and a box of gloves, he lined up the ten students and guided them through the procedure from insertion to withdrawal of the digit.

I gathered that seven days later there was a complaint raised from one of the students, not about the rectal exam but that he'd been offered dinner that evening. The invitation had come while performing the procedure, suggesting to me considerable digital expertise.

SanAntonio's direct feedback on prostate pressure was probably well intentioned, but the dean of the medical school felt he'd shown a little too much commitment to his students, so he was taken off the course for the rest of that term, only to re-emerge later on in the course and again when my fellowship exam took place a decade later.

In my first clinical skills class, we were taught to feel the pulse of the heart through the chest wall and were asked to locate the position of the apex beat, where the ventricle reached its lowest point, and tap on the chest wall. In a more buxom lady, possessing a larger-than-average bosom, this entailed lifting the breast with one hand to enable the stethoscope to be placed in the correct position. The very first patient I examined as a medical student was a 46 FFF. I'd never handled a breast, large or small, before. Moving hers was like trying to tame a living blancmange the size of a basketball. What lay beneath hadn't seen daylight in two decades. It was with great reluctance that I used my hand to feel the apex beat followed by positioning my virgin stethoscope to listen to the heart.

The stethoscope never felt the same again. Camembert cheese always brought that day back to me whenever I smelled it.

I should add that ever since qualifying as a doctor I never felt another apex beat and was fairly sure it wasn't to the detriment of any patient to avoid this. Quite soon, I learned I had an aversion to putting my fingers in damp places, particularly the armpit, where the smell lingered on your fingers and reminded you of the experience while eating a sandwich at lunch.

# 16

# Personality Test

## September 2003

Twenty or so years on from my time dealing with prostates and apex beats, I decided to undertake a higher degree — a master of education, to be specific. I felt it might open some new doors and opportunities for me.

The course involved three days every few weeks of in-person lectures, with projects to complete at home in between. There were fifteen of us in the course, and naturally I found it hard to find anything in common with any of them. Catherine told me once again that I could at least try to make an effort at friendliness. I told her that was nonsense; it was normal to hold a general dislike of human beings. Perhaps the abnormal person was the one who was full of bonhomie upon meeting me, grinning idiotically and laughing at weak jokes. That always put me on my guard. Those folks became salespeople. The worst went on to be pharma representatives.

In the first half-hour of the course, the lecturer, a socialist Welsh nationalist in her fifties who seemed to hate humans even more than I did, had already used words such as *epistemology*, which I didn't understand, though I wrote them down determined to include them in my first assignment. She told us all humans learned in different ways and then spent the next hour explaining that all the old ways of teaching were wrong.

The other fourteen in the course nodded sagely, which made me dislike them even more. The lecturer started rattling on about the nature of truth and knowledge, and I soon found my mind wandering away from the task at hand, totally missing her rant about the English as I recalled Catherine's wrath when I'd left the day before for the course.

I was in the doghouse once again. Catherine had found a cleaner that apparently made floors shine like brand-new. She'd cleaned all the kitchen and hall tiles, and we were going to go out as a family for a dog walk and pub lunch. It was going to be grim, since the rain had just started. We were all in the car when I realized I'd left the car keys in the kitchen, so I ran into the house to get them.

By the time I reached the house, my walking boots were of the perfect wetness to transfer muddy footprints with every step through the hall and into the kitchen. As I turned around, keys in hand, I spotted the disaster. Then I had the brilliant idea to put a tea towel under each boot and "skate" back to the front door, simultaneously cleaning and polishing while removing the evidence. It seemed to me to do the trick. When I reached the doormat, I picked up the two tea towels and put them in the back of the cupboard by the front door. I was pleased with the result, and by the time we drove half a mile, I totally forgot the whole thing.

Upon our return, Catherine spotted the sin within approximately four seconds, and in another five, she discovered the dirty tea towels. This was one of those crimes in which the sentence was unclear but involved a lot of meaningful looks and a vaguely unsettling atmosphere. Then I made a half-hearted attempt to look for the floor mop but searched in the wrong places, compounding the problem further.

Suddenly, though, I was back in the course and realized everybody around me was engaged in hunting for a document that had been handed out to all of us while I was daydreaming. It was a personality test. I hadn't actually ever heard of this before, but I could see it involved completing a questionnaire with about a hundred banal statements where the right answer was clear. Mainly, you had to strongly agree, agree, disagree, or strongly disagree with each statement. Things like "I enjoy meeting new people" or "I avoid conflict in the workplace."

I couldn't imagine other people having quite such a different world view than I had. But on presenting the results, the other fourteen in the course had wildly different answers. I began to realize why I was struggling to engage with them. Essentially, they all had distorted, incorrect views of the world. The challenge I faced, however, was that even looking back at my answers, I struggled to see how the others could have gotten the answers so wrong.

That was it. Perhaps a master's in education wasn't for me, though I decided to give it one more month.

# 17

# ORGASMIA

## APRIL 2002

About once every ten years a new disease was discovered. Strangely, new diseases were more likely to gain traction when there was a treatment available with a recent secure patent. I noticed lately that many of my patients were asking me to prescribe Orgasmia, a new treatment from Plus Denario Pharmaceuticals for Powel Syndrome. At least once a day one of my patients asked if they could have it.

I had an old school friend who worked in middle management at Plus Denario, and what follows is the verbatim account he told me about concerning one of the meetings that led to his firm's new blockbuster drug.

The process started during one of Denario's three monthly "Corporate Blue Sky Thinking" (CBST) meetings in which upper and middle management got together to discuss current actively marketed drugs, drugs in the pipeline, and marketing strategy.

Bob Skelton chaired the meeting and encouraged all employees in the room to describe their ideas on how Denario could increase its share of the market. Guy Benfield, who struggled to take his job as seriously as he might, suggested that Denario needed to expand its current portfolio, preferably with a low-risk drug for a common problem.

"What sort of problem are you thinking about?" asked Skelton.

"I'm really not sure," replied Guy. "But we're here today to think outside the box. Let's synergize and start to pick the low-hanging fruit. Then we can circle back."

Strangely, everybody else in the meeting seemed to understand what he was saying.

"Get the whiteboards," urged Lucy Catton, who organized the CBST meetings and whose job title was primary assistant to the future portfolio development marketing sub-manager. "Who wants to be the scribe?"

A couple of product managers, always fearful about the security of their jobs, eagerly leaped up and grabbed marker pens in two colours, ready to jot down the pearls coming out of the blue-sky bonanza.

Vikram Chowdhry, the medical science liaison, piped up. "Preferably, any study would have fairly dubious outcome measures difficult to prove or disprove. The more subjective the better. Also, preferably the drug would tend to be at the homeopathic end of the spectrum, since self-evidently we wouldn't want too many adverse effects. The Nothrombo data last year took months to re-create to make it look meaningful. And I'm still dreading someone reviewing the cardiac adverse event data."

Crystal Rowe, senior pharmacologist, added, "I suggest the target population should probably be unhappy females in their thirties who are overly attentive to their own health with a range of subjective symptoms."

"Such as what?" asked Skelton.

From around the room came various suggestions, including tingling, brain fog, dropping things. The scribes frantically added low libido, bloating, and occasional blurred vision. One scribe even heard a *sotto voce* comment that most of the target group might just be pissed off with life, and there were the four words in green marked for everyone to see on the whiteboard.

Things went on this way for quite a while.

"How about Neuro-abdo-vagino-hormonal Syndrome," offered Vikram. "We could call it NAVAHO."

"That might upset Indigenous people in America," someone pointed out.

Crystal smiled. "What about Heaven Syndrome?"

"That one's taken," a marketing person insisted.

"Wait!" shouted Skelton. "I've got it. Look!" He walked over to the whiteboard and read, "Pissed off with life. POWL Syndrome."

Jessie Flintoff, secondary assistant to the future portfolio development marketing sub-manager, quickly came up with an interesting idea. About eight years earlier, Plus Denario Pharmaceuticals had created a placebo for a trial for a new heart medication. The plan was that five hundred patients would get the active drug in the trial and another five hundred would get the placebo.

The trial was stopped early because most of the patients in the active treatment group felt considerably worse, but in the placebo group not only were they unchanged but a fair percentage of patients also felt a great deal better. It transpired that a sister company of Denario that made a range of automotive fluids had provided the base chemicals for the placebo, including a patented sugar molecule used to stabilize antifreeze. Although the trial was terminated, the new molecule maintained its intellectual copyright and was filed away for potential future use.

"It's harmless, useless, and safe," said Jessie, her voice rising in excitement. "And with a bit of work, we can make the data statistically significant."

Bill Sharpe, the head of marketing and a heavy smoker, heavy drinker, and bon viveur, was already on board. "How about we get Professor Powel from St. Benedict's Hospital to invent the syndrome using his name. I reckon if we pay him enough, he'll talk about this across the country and help us design the trials. Nobody needs to know how we came up with the name." He was on a roll now. "We'll get a contract research organization to do the studies. They can choose a location that'll give us the best outcomes. I'm thinking Eastern Europe or India — easier to get through the Ethics Board. We can get phase one and two studies done pretty fast, since we know the molecule's safe. Remember what they say — 'there are no drugs, there are just molecules with data attached to them.' Then another few hundred thousand pounds to send doctors to advisory boards to 'ask their advice' will seal the deal. If we pay those doctors £3,000 each to sit and listen to us talking about the new drug, they'll soon be prescribing it."

"Don't forget we'll need some patient advocates," suggested Val Probert, one of the company lawyers whose primary role was to find legal ways to extend patents and who had the scruples of a hungry fox. "My sister works for *Cosmopolitan* magazine. I'll get her to gather some patient stories and it'll trend like wildfire."

And so ended the first meeting. A team was hastily assembled to design the studies, and suitably motivated physicians were found to conduct them for a fee. The best part of drug trials was that most of the work could be done by a contract research organization, while most, or all, of the statistical analysis could be handled by a publication team and in-house statisticians. The physician of the final published paper would do very little, sometimes almost zero, of the real work, but his or her name was what mattered. Once the paper was ready for publication, the Ethics Board would again become a little flexible, since the journal editor scoped out how to coordinate publishing the paper with well-placed advertisements in the same journal, and probably a journal supplement paid for by Plus Denario. Working with Big Pharma as a journal editor could also be a moneymaker if done carefully.

Professor Powel quickly agreed that this new syndrome was a terrible affliction. He even came up with the Powel Score, a single number in which all the vague symptoms could be scored together, each out of three, added together, divided by 8.34, and the number was arrived at. It would make the data so much harder to interpret, which was exactly what the pharmaceutical company required.

The training manager was immediately called upon to design the reps training program. The marketers created the advertisements that appeared in the medical journals, and a North America–wide TV commercial was developed, featuring a cast member of a sitcom from the 1990s who claimed to have Powel Syndrome. The industry knew a celebrity was essential to help market a disease and its treatment. A mere four years on, Orgasmia was available by private prescription only, and such was the demand, Plus Denario had to slow down availability to ensure ongoing fervour in the press.

The reps were sent out in force to visit general practitioners and hospital doctors. Marketing materials featured attractive couples looking as if Orgasmia had saved their marriages, as well as a smaller picture of an older couple holding hands gazing at the sunset after what the reader assumed was a long walk along the sand. There were also a few graphs for the doctors who pretended to understand statistics, of which only five percent actually did, and a script from the rep for the super-clever-dick doctor who asked too many questions about how what was essentially sugar could possibly be effective.

"If you have a doctor who pretends to be intellectual," announced the training manager, "just mention carbon chains and unique hydroxyl molecules and most will shut up. If they keep going, ask them to be a speaker at a meeting."

Next would come the phone surveys. There were various companies that conducted them on behalf of the pharmaceutical industry. They generally followed the same strategy. First of all, doctors were asked what particular diseases they looked after and what drugs they were familiar with for those conditions.

In the second part of the interview, the survey people returned to the lists of drugs previously mentioned and asked the doctors a series of questions, usually six to eight, about the specific drug and then went on to the next on the list. It didn't take long for the doctors to realize that the best way to take part in these surveys was to only recall a maximum of two drugs for any condition because they'd get the same fee and the survey would take forty minutes less. An added nuance was that you needed to know who was funding the survey, since remembering to mention that company's drug encouraged it to ask you to complete future surveys. Everybody did the same thing, the net result being that all of these telephone surveys were completely useless and produced whatever answers a pharmaceutical company wanted.

# 18

# Communication Skills

## October 23, 2004

The day started badly. I decided to use some initiative and made the bed. About five minutes later, Catherine came in and pulled all the sheets off. "Surely, you know by now that Saturday's the day we change the sheets," she told me.

I had no idea that was the case.

It was two days since I'd hidden the skeleton in the footings on Morris Furniss's extension. No construction workers had turned up on the Friday, so I assumed it would be Monday before the skeleton was discovered.

For those who recalled the days of Saturday night entertainment in the 1970s, the sight of magicians pulling out seemingly endless strings of ribbons from their pockets should be familiar. I was reliving this trick with our dog, who had somehow swallowed grass. A small amount, one inch, protruded from its anus. Catherine's face made it clear that it was up to me to don the washing-up gloves and remove the grass, which was clearly distressing the creature and was disturbing me, too, since the grass had already left marks on our unnecessarily cream living room rug.

It would be no exaggeration to state that somehow the grass had knitted together inside the dog. The plant material I extracted was at least twenty inches long, and I was still holding it in my yellow rubber gloves when my mother-in-law entered the utility room wearing a dressing gown and, oddly, holding my electric razor.

"I just needed to do a little landscaping down below," she explained. "Don't worry. I did clean it."

She passed the razor to me. I noted at least two grey pubic hairs caught in the blades. That didn't really worry me. I was going to buy a new one today.

Being Saturday, I couldn't even choose to leave the house and seek refuge at work. With Catherine's parents in our home, the only option was to do some studying for my master's degree in education, which I was still plodding away at.

I was hoping I could somehow incorporate the master's coursework into my job, killing two birds with one stone. For the research project component of the degree, I elected to examine communication, more specifically how patients got their information. As such, I had one of those Archimedes-in-the-bath moments.

**Question 1:** Where do your patients find reliable information about their conditions?

**Answer:**

1. Family doctor.
2. Specialist.
3. Internet.
4. Local patient group.
5. The hairdresser.

**Question 2:** When your patients need steroids to reduce the disease activity, who do they listen to?

**Answer:**

1. Partner.
2. Family doctor.
3. Specialist.
4. Internet.
5. The hairdresser.

**Question 3:** When your patients develop a mysterious rash, who knows the correct diagnosis?

**Answer:**

1. Dermatologist.
2. Family doctor.
3. Internet.
4. A friend in the canteen who had another friend whose mother had a similar rash.
5. The hairdresser.

Judging by the answers I got, there was a pattern here: doctors weren't the most trusted persons patients talk to. I had no doubt that despite honing my communication skills, reading two medical journals a month, attending conferences, and taking care of patients for twenty years, all of my knowledge and experience could be undermined by a single sentence from a hairdresser, since she or he possessed some sort of mysterious credibility that most doctors could only dream of.

When Sharon, while applying a hair dye, stated, "My friend's dad went on to steroids and died four days later," the client would go home and flush the pills down the toilet. Not mentioned was that the friend's dad was taking steroids for asthma and had actually died falling off a ladder when cleaning bird muck from his bedroom window.

While trimming hair around the ears, the hairdresser would say, "You mustn't agree to having that procedure [insert any procedure here]. My friend, Natasha, had that and she can't even go back to work now. And one boob is bigger than the other. *Oooh*, that rash is nasty. You know what it is? It's a fungal rash. Have you got a dog? It's ringworm."

Sometimes the hairdresser's colleague, who did nails, would agree.

The last comments about rashes could apply to every skin problem: eczema, psoriasis, and most skin tumours.

On the subject of communication yesterday, Friday, Professor Sir Desmond Leech, OBE, was the hot topic this week. The hospital rumour mill, the medical secretary telegraph system, had discovered he'd had another major shouting match during a procedure to remove part of the colon. Apparently, he asked for a clamp and was given scissors, resulting in him cutting straight through a major blood vessel. His trainee backed the professor, while the scrub nurse and anesthetist told the opposite story. Since the anesthetist was completing a crossword at the time, her reliability was in some doubt.

Leech marched out of the operating theatre, leaving his trainee to finish off. He threw his latex gloves into the corner at one of the nurses, who burst into tears when he told her she should be fired as he left. Calmer heads suggested we let everybody cool off, since there seemed no joy in a he-said-she-said style of complaint. The fate of the patient wasn't mentioned in all of this gossip, but I assumed everything ended up well. One thing was certain: Mother Nature healed many patients despite attempts by the medical profession to finish them off.

Meanwhile, I was in conversation with Nigel Robinson, king of innuendo, who had just admitted a man to Ward 8 with shortness of breath after a road traffic accident. The story, as related to me, was that he and his girlfriend had decided, while driving eighty miles per hour down the motorway, that they needed some diversion to offer relief from the boredom of the journey.

Nigel laughed. "I think it arose after she suggested he pull off at the next junction. I guess he misinterpreted the instruction."

Suffice to say, the man then tried to raise the steering wheel while driving in the fast lane to achieve what Nigel described as "more head room." The next thing the patient remembered was waking in the ambulance. The girlfriend miraculously cheated death but was in a following ambulance with the indicator stick piercing her cheek as if she were a kebab.

# 19

# A Joyous Union Announced

## June 2004

Horror of horrors — our niece was getting married. That should be a time of joy and family unity. The coming together of two families to make one. A wonderful opportunity to reunite with distant relatives and catch up on their lives. A celebration of a beautiful couple as they embarked on a journey together. So why did I feel so negative?

Firstly, Catherine's sister's children were ghastly. They seemed to have minimal manners and were about as interesting as stones. The daughter's name was Sunshine, but she looked anything but. She had constantly greasy hair and a large ring hanging from the middle of her nose that reminded me that she should be on display at a county agriculture fair. Worse, the niece mooched around our house and always wore tops that displayed her slightly hairy umbilicus as it oozed over her jeans like a bowl of rising dough.

Somehow she managed to find a chain-smoking mute who adored her. His name was Kevin, but he was known as Spider because he had a very artistic tattoo of a web arising from his chest and encircling his neck. In four months' time, this blossoming love was going to be officially recognized in St. Mary's Parish in a church where Sunshine had never stepped. What joy coursed through my veins when I imagined the union of these two beautiful souls and their subsequent progeny.

I could picture the pain of talking to other people I didn't know and didn't ever wish to know in the clubhouse of the local Rugby Club during the reception. Undoubtedly, there would be melon balls as a starter. I suspected the rest would be inedible, since they'd roped in Edith from the post office to roast some meat on Spider's barbecue, which I was to take down the evening before. Spider's father had agreed that our friend, Patrick, would brew a special elderberry wine for the occasion.

The whole affair was going to cost us a fortune. I'd need a new suit; my current one seemed to have shrunk by two inches around the waist. Catherine would have to buy a hat, which she'd only ever wear once, partly because it would be so awful and partly because it would get lost during the reception. We'd also need to stay in a hotel. I'd already worked out that this wedding would cost more than our annual holiday. And we'd have to get a present, of course. My initial budget for the gift was £20, but the couple-to-be sent us a link to a website with a list of what they wanted guests to buy them.

I scanned the right-hand column of the list and realized I was too late to get the three cheapest items, leaving the fourth cheapest, a set of Wedgwood dinner plates. Wedgwood? Really? This couple had spent the past decade eating fried chicken out of a cardboard box!

Catherine, meanwhile, was very excited and even chatting away to her sister about table decorations and some sort of pillowcase thing to put over the chairs in the Rugby Club to make it seem like the Savoy Hotel. I knew where that was going: I'd be roped into some time-consuming activity and Catherine would agree to bake a cake, which meant seven cakes until she was happy with the result.

Nevertheless, we emailed back to accept the invitation and express our considerable excitement.

# 20

# Missing Person

## October 24, 2004

Catherine's parents were incapable of a quick departure. Instead, they prolonged the leaving process for about forty minutes. So I decided at 4:00 p.m. to walk the dog. To my dismay, I saw the builder's van outside the Furniss residence. I figured Morris had come to check on the footings prior to the concrete pour the next day. When I spotted the builder poking at the object I'd seen being rolled into the footings a few days earlier, I kept walking and devised a circular route so I wouldn't return the same way. When I returned, I was delighted to see that Catherine's parents had left. That pleasure was quickly extinguished when I saw what awaited me.

On the kitchen table sat the plastic bag I'd thrown into the attic the previous Thursday. Catherine eyed me suspiciously, ready to shine a bright light into my eyes and ask why there was a black balaclava in the far corner of the loft.

"Do you think the previous owner was a member of the IRA?" she asked.

I almost laughed with relief. I hadn't been discovered. "Dev Singh?" I replied. "He never struck me as IRA."

I was saved by the bell! The phone started ringing, and I eagerly rushed to answer it rather than be caught lying about the balaclava.

But it stopped ringing before I picked up. I listened to the message. It was Norm, the Milky Bar Kid. He'd left a message telling us that his mother, the medium, was missing. Could I call him back as soon as possible?

When I got him on the phone, he told me he was very anxious that he hadn't seen his mother for a few days. I couldn't get much more sense from him, and Catherine, sensing an opportunity, suggested that rather than prepare food tonight we have cod and chips. That way I could pop into the apartment above the Silver Cod to see Milky while the order was being cooked and find out what was going on. Norm eagerly agreed and asked me to let myself in, since the doorbell was faulty.

I drove down through the regular fine drizzle of Kilminster, and ten minutes later was parked outside the Silver Cod, finding myself behind the same white van I'd seen the previous day parked near Morris Furniss's house. Standing nearby in a black hoodie was a young man I vaguely recognized who couldn't have looked any shiftier if he'd tried. He looked straight at me and bolted off down the street.

Strolling into the takeaway, I placed my order. The Silver Cod wasn't what it used to be. Formerly, there was always constant banter between the owner and his customers. Now there was a morgue-like silence. I'd known the establishment ever since it had opened. Recently, the shop had changed hands, though the previous owner, Greg Hobson, continued to do the frying.

"Evening, Greg," I said to him over the counter. "Cod and chips twice, please. I'm surprised to see you here. I thought when you sold up you were going to take early retirement and travel the globe."

"Actually, I didn't sell. I just have two colleagues now who have taken over the management." He indicated a scary, seemingly East European giant, possibly Romanian, whom I could just glimpse through the back of the shop and then glanced down to another six-foot-six goliath waiting for an order. Come to think of it, I'd noticed the same man in the same chair two previous times. He, too, looked suspiciously like a foreigner, I reflected.

"I hardly think you needed help," I said. "After all, you built this place up from nothing. I still remember it when it was a launderette."

Greg gave me a weary smile. The man in the chair, who looked like a nightclub bouncer, stood to collect his order. I suspected something else was going on here. I'd heard Catherine saying she thought Greg had gambling debts. Maybe this was why he'd found himself partners to manage the business.

While my cod was frying, I stepped out into the drizzle again through the misted-up glass door of the takeaway and headed next door to Milky's apartment and his mother's spiritual operation, which were above the Silver Cod. On the downstairs red door was a hastily written card stating in garbled English that all Tarot readings and spiritual connections were cancelled until further notice DUE TOO UNFOURSCENE CURCUMSTANCES ALL APPOINTMENTS THIS WEAK ARE CANCELED.

I climbed the stairs of the somewhat fusty home that smelled like unemptied cat litter, damp, and fried cod. At the top, I heard the loud buzz from the pump in the old aquarium and called Norm's name. "Milky, it's me, Brian."

"Through here," he replied.

I walked into the mystical room where Milky's mother consulted her clients. He was sitting there gazing into the crystal ball in the centre of the table. The room had wooden floorboards and would have benefited from an area rug, especially since there was a large dark stain just to the right of the table.

"Mum's disappeared," he started.

"What do you mean, disappeared?"

"She vanished a couple of days ago."

"Did she take anything with her?" I'd seen enough police dramas to know the kind of questions to ask.

He looked slightly surprised at my query but told me he hadn't looked and wasn't sure how he'd know.

"Well, for example, is her toothbrush still there? Did she take her phone?" Then I added, "Have you called the police?"

"Do you think I should?"

By this stage, he'd developed a sheen of sweat across his face and a marked tremor in both hands. My sense was that he was confabulating, since he stuttered out some implausible reason why he hadn't contacted them. "Maybe she's just gone on holiday," he suggested.

"I hardly think she'd just disappear. Didn't you tell me she was fully booked all week?" The other clue that he was being less than frank with me was that, as he was talking to me, his phone rang and the caller ID said "Mum."

Norm answered the phone, saying, "Hi, Gordon. It's Milky here," as if the caller didn't know whom they'd called. "I'm just with Brian Standish. I'll call you right back."

He ended the call. I felt like asking him if "Gordon" actually knew me, but since I was a skillful sleuth, I said nothing. I'd ask Catherine what she made of all this but suggested to Milky once more that he call the police. However, he still seemed highly reluctant to do so, and halfway through our conversation, he suddenly decided he knew exactly where she was — in Wales visiting a friend.

Luckily for Milky, I knew my cod and chips must be ready and promised to call him later. For the time being, he was off the hook. As I descended the stairs, I tried to imagine why he was making a great, though implausible, pretense that his mother was missing. Did she owe money? Had she committed a crime? And if he knew, then why had he phoned me in the first place?

Once outside Milky's, I walked straight into the man in the dark hoodie. This time I recognized him as one of the nurses from Kilminster General. I wished him a good evening, and he stared back at me, petrified.

As I pulled into the driveway with our dinner, I noticed two police cars parked outside Morris Furniss's home. One had its blue lights flashing. Within ten minutes, the police were joined by two ambulances and two more squad cars.

I imagined that if the police decided to ask the neighbours if they'd seen any suspicious activity and then confronted me, I'd immediately fall to the floor weeping and ask for forgiveness. So, it was important for me to practise looking innocent. I stood in front of the hall mirror, trying to put on the face of someone who hadn't left an antique skeleton in some footings.

# 21

# The Three Wise Men

## October 25, 2004

Monday morning started disappointingly. I decided to clean the toilet and did a pretty good job in my opinion, even scrubbing the outside of the bowl. To finish off, I left a lot of blue stuff in the bowl, the better to make it clear I'd played my part in the running of the house. Admittedly, that feeling was a little deflated when Catherine didn't notice my hard work. So, over supper, I said, "You won't need to clean the hall toilet. I did it earlier."

"What do you want? A medal? I've cleaned it for the past ten years."

Catherine then reeled off a list of household tasks completed each week without her having to tell me. Obviously, it was a mistake on my part to have cleaned the toilet, so silently, I vowed to steer clear of household chores for a while.

When I got to the hospital, I headed to the clinic to do my shift. Halfway there, our chief executive officer spotted me and asked if I could spare five minutes. Of course, I agreed. Unlike ninety-nine percent of hospital CEOs, she was completely delightful, mainly because she took a hands-off approach and let everybody get on with their business, preferring to drink green tea and share the macarons she'd made the evening before. She wasn't an intellectual heavyweight by any means, but she led her team well. I suspected they enjoyed the fact they could pretty much do as they liked as long as the financial bottom line and the current targets were met. So, we made our way to her office.

Not many staff members knew that the CEO also had a claim to fame. She'd been a winner in *The Generation Game* in 1976. Her husband had left home for five weeks after her victory because during the final part, in which she had to remember a number of items passing before her on a conveyor belt, she failed to recall a single one. The host, Bruce Forsythe, helpful as always, reminded her of several, so she went home with a fondue set, a pair of deck chairs, a lava lamp, and a cuddly toy. I noted that the photograph of Mrs. Macaron holding her fondue set, Bruce with his arm around her shoulders, decorated the wall of her office.

When we were comfortably seated in her office, she explained, "I'm not totally sure what's going on, but I'm worried they're going to make me into an escape goat."

"An escape goat?" I echoed.

"Yes, you know how it is in hospitals. The managers get the blame for everything. And frankly, I want this to go away. Things have been pretty good since the Jeremiah Foch incident, other than when that hooligan let off three fire distinguishers in the foyer."

She stopped awkwardly, suddenly remembering that Jeremiah had been alive as the elevator doors closed and dead as they opened on the next floor, with Richard Headley and me walking out and leaving the corpse, the lift doors closing, hitting his shoe, and opening again, until the police had arrived. To be fair, Jeremiah had had a cardiac arrest in the elevator, though since the doors were closed, the half-hearted attempt at resuscitation was witnessed by nobody. This was, after all, the man who had murdered several of my colleagues. He'd been unmarried, with no children, which made things marginally less distressing, though his sister, who apparently shared the same calorie-intake to calories-burnt ratio as Jeremiah, had vehemently argued that her brother was innocent of the crimes for which he never faced justice.

The administrative structure divided Mrs. Macaron's team into medical and surgical specialities, along with laboratory services and radiology. The new medical specialities manager was a young woman who looked as if she was on a work experience day from her high school. She'd taken over from the late Jeremiah Foch whose enthusiasm for promotion and visceral hatred of the medical profession were both typical of the role, and in his case ultimately fatal to several doctors and himself. I gathered that the new medical specialities manager's qualification for the role was that she'd managed to improve the efficiency of ordering milk and cheese for the canteen by identifying a different supplier, who by great coincidence was her brother.

The surgical manager, Danny Flowers, was already trained to despise the doctors he managed, so he was well placed to succeed in his role. However, the CEO explained to me that Danny was struggling with a sensitive issue.

I assumed perhaps she meant a syphilitic chancre on his penis, or maybe prolapsed hemorrhoids.

"Him and me have a problem that requires careful handling," the CEO continued, grammar being one of her weaknesses, more than balanced by her kindness and expertise in making macarons.

"I have to be honest," I said. "I'd describe myself as being somewhat ambivalent about management roles."

"Oh, good. Danny said he didn't think you would have strong feelings one way or the other. I just feel we need to deal with this as quietly as possible. The surgical nurses are making a lot of noise about it, and I think this is just exasperating the situation. I definitely don't want any of his patients to think we have a rogue doctor. But I believe you need to look beyond the gossip and find something Pacific."

She had lost me by this point. "Pacific?" I queried.

"Yes, something more than just rumour."

I'd initially imagined the rogue doctor would be the master of innuendo and lavatorial filth, Nigel Robinson, but he wouldn't be part of the surgical team. Therefore, I suspected one of the junior doctors was the likely issue. After all, it hadn't been more than a year since the embarrassing case of Marigold Chang.

She was an eleventh-hour appointment to fill an unpopular surgical junior doctor post with our urologist, Gerrit Van der Walt.

The new academic year was due to start in forty-eight hours and there had been zero applicants. Just as we were going to be compelled to alter the on-call rotations, Marigold submitted her application. She sent in her excellent curriculum vitae describing honours at the medical school in Brisbane, Australia, followed by a break from medicine to complete a Ph.D. Marigold even included a précis of her Ph.D. dissertation, which described laboratory research on bladder innervation.

While academically an elite doctor, Chang proved somewhat less useful clinically. She'd surprisingly passed the English-language requirements for registration. Surprising because nobody could understand what she was saying. Her patient assessments made little sense, and on her first weekend on call, she ordered transfusions for most patients whether they needed them or not and failed to properly cross-match the samples, resulting in one patient spending the next week in intensive care.

Gerrit Van der Walt thought she was excellent, but one had to remember this was the first person in twelve years to apply for his post. He gave her excellent three-month appraisals and thus she continued in her job.

About six weeks later, we employed a locum doctor for a different position, who by total chance happened to have graduated from the same Brisbane medical school in the same year as Marigold. He claimed never to have seen her before in his life. At that point, the hospital chased up the referees, which at the time of offering her the role had been overlooked, such was the relief felt in the medical staffing office. A brief search of the literature in the hospital library revealed her Ph.D. had been plagiarized.

Marigold was challenged, of course, but disappeared, never to be seen again, before anybody considered calling the police. Teams above my pay grade were left to decide how far to pursue the issue, and nothing more was ever mentioned. I wasn't even sure if somebody had decided this was too embarrassing to be made public, but surely our noble leaders would never make a decision purely because it might put their own futures in jeopardy.

I thought of asking the CEO if the concerns related to junior doctors were worth the bother, since nowadays it took considerably less effort to allow such persons an average pass on their training rotations than have to go through the multiple appeals, grievances, and eventual legal proceedings that would result if it was suggested the juniors weren't as good as they believed they were.

Certainly, there were a thousand things more palatable to me than getting involved in managing a hospital complaint. Dysentery, for example.

"You haven't even told me who this is about," I finally said. "I'm assuming it's one of the surgical trainees. I think you need to gather some data and ask the medical director to advise us on what to do. Isn't there something called the 'Three Wise Men' to advise on tricky situations? There will be a process defined that we could follow." I cursed myself for saying *we*.

The CEO frowned. "Well, that's the problem. This is about the medical director."

I was momentarily lost for words. A battle with Professor Sir Desmond Leech? "Professor … Leech?" I stammered.

I rather wished I hadn't allowed myself to be flattered in to accepting this role. I had agreed, only to learn that it involved an unwinnable, certain conflict with colleagues — precisely the reason I'd left health care the first time around.

She told me she'd ask Danny to meet with me to discuss Pacific details.

Apologizing to her, I said I had to get myself to the clinic. I'd only walked three steps when she stopped me, gave me a knowing look, and lifted her bag to retrieve something. Transfixed, I knew what was coming. My mouth started to water. She was going to give me some macarons — a perfect mid-morning snack. I began to smile.

But she pulled out a piece of paper and unfolded it. "I'm doing a sponsored baking event. People are sponsoring me per macaron. I don't suppose you mind, do you?"

Never had I felt so deflated and ambushed. "How many do you think you're going to make?"

"Oh, probably about a hundred."

"And who's the money going to?"

"I'm trying to raise money to take the middle managers on a team-building trip to Chessington World of Adventures."

I was hard-pressed to think of any less worthy cause than this. Wavering, I began to formulate the words to politely decline her offer. But she interrupted my thoughts, saying that almost every other member of the medical department was already sponsoring her, so with the deepest regret, I accepted her offer.

Quickly, I scanned the names on the sheet and the amount they were offering. I saw no name I recognized but didn't want to lowball her. Yet I wanted to sit safely in the middle of the pack, so I smiled like a tetanus victim as I parted with another £20.

When I was finished my clinic shift, I arrived home to a very excited Catherine who had been chatting to the wife of one of the police officers involved in the Furniss case.

"There are two bodies," she told me. "One's a middle-aged female, as yet unidentified, and the other's an older body. I think they believe this is the work of a serial killer."

"What? One body and an old skeleton."

She failed to pick up my obvious mistake and carried on breathlessly. "I was thinking. Could Milky's missing mom could be the dead woman?"

I felt this was unlikely. "Well, I suspect they'll identify her from her dental records. Though how in heaven's name they'll know who her dentist is I have no idea."

# 22

# Dementors

## October 26, 2004

I'd heard nothing more about the bodies in the footings case, but I could barely concentrate, assuming every knock at my door was a group of armed police officers ready to storm in and pin me to the floor.

Coming back to a job in health care after a week or two of vacation was always like returning to an abusive relationship. But trying to perform when there were other things on one's mind made it even harder. Sometimes patients forgot their doctor had problems, too.

Running clinics at present was proving challenging. My mind, rarely able to focus for long, kept wandering back to prison cells and unrequested shower buggery.

I wondered if my patients could see the thoughts behind my smiling face. Before the first series of Kilminster murders, I could safely say that most of the time, if I was able to concentrate, I was usually genuinely interested and empathetic. But since that time, and particularly in the past week or so, I was struggling to focus, and a patient could talk to me for five minutes while I just heard white noise.

Those familiar with Harry Potter should know that one of his arch-enemies was the dementor, that frightening creature who sucked all joy from one's soul. Nora Guthrie was a dementor. Try as

I might, when I saw her name on a clinic list, I was filled with dismay in the certain knowledge that I faced thirty minutes of utter misery as she regaled me with every negative story about her own health and also that of friends and relatives. Cystitis was a particular favourite. As long as her stories involved death or cancer, she could keep on going in a rather disconcertingly high voice that brought to mind Mickey Mouse. Nora was number four on my Rocket List.

I should clarify. Most people were familiar with the concept of a Bucket List: the ten things to do before one died. Perhaps less familiar to patients was the concept of the Rocket List: ten patients one would gladly launch into space, smiling as they blasted off into orbit, never to be seen again or, if particularly lucky, to hear they'd burnt up upon re-entry.

I'd arranged for a nurse to come into the clinic room after twelve minutes to ask me to attend an emergency. After a quarter of an hour, she still hadn't rescued me, and by twenty minutes, I realized I was destined once again to have the last vestiges of joy removed from my already withering body as I listened to the story of Nora's neighbour whose daughter's friend had defied diagnosis by seven doctors but had finally been told by a nutritionist that it was because she wasn't eating enough fermented cabbage, which contained some mysterious essential element.

As my soul began to escape my earthly remains, the nurse finally came in, fifteen minutes later than planned, asking me to attend a patient on Ward 3 immediately. I made an excellent show of leaping up and rushing out, whereupon I hid in a storeroom until Nora had left the clinic. Broken but ready for another two hours of clinic after a reviving chocolate digestive biscuit, I was also reassured that no police officers had been seen in the outpatient department searching for me.

When I finished my morning clinic, I headed back to my office where a peanut-butter-and-Marmite sandwich Catherine had made that morning awaited. I was looking forward to thirty minutes with my feet up on the desk listening to some Electric Light Orchestra. Danny Flowers was due to meet me in half an hour. He was currently organizing a visit from an Australian TV celebrity due to open the new pediatric wing. Little did Danny know that a new expression, "to be cancelled," would lead to the wing being renamed a decade later.

Thus, I was disappointed when I entered my office and saw Adrian O'Dell, the drug representative for Janrex Pharmaceuticals. My secretary had let him into the office, and he was laying out a range of promotional materials on my desk, along with a pile of patient education pamphlets, all heavily branded and which would find themselves in the trash in half an hour. He was delighted to see me, grinning at me and pumping my hand as if we were old school friends.

"So great to see you, Brian," he gushed.

First-name terms? I'd only met him once before.

I didn't have any antipathy toward Adrian. However, the role of drug rep required a high level of false bonhomie and sycophancy. However much reps positioned themselves as my greatest fan and friend, I had to remember they were just doing a job. The reality was they probably didn't like me at all. In the world of pharma sales, that was known as detailing the doctor.

In my specialty, the reps' strategy initially involved them asking me how I chose my anticoagulant, hanging on to my words as if I were providing ultimate wisdom. What actually was happening was that I was being flattered into imagining my opinion had value. That flattery was meant to persuade me to feel positive toward Janrex Pharmaceuticals.

Adrian's provision of a sandwich sealed the contract, since I was then forced to look at a few bar charts purporting to show the difference between the chosen drug and the nearest competitors. The details on these graphs were always hard for me to understand other than that the lines were far apart, so the easiest option was to murmur in wonder at the impressive *p* value that a medical school lecture eons ago described as the statistic confirming the study results were significant. Epidemiology and statistics weren't my forte, so I was easy to con.

I gathered some companies categorized doctors as characters from Winnie-the-Pooh and offered training strategies to optimize the outcome for the different personalities. I had no doubt I was Eeyore.

Other pharmaceutical firms labelled doctors as members of the British Royal Family. If I was Prince Harry, I wouldn't think overly deeply and would flit from drug to drug. If I was Prince Charles, I might be hard to convince to change my preferred drug, since I likely would adopt a measured traditional approach. Quite by chance, I discovered I was the Duke of Edinburgh, which suited me fine. He'd always been one of my heroes. Frankly, it was a relief not to be Prince Andrew.

Danny Flowers turned up at the exact time of our appointment in my office to discuss the "sensitive problem." This allowed me to sadly terminate my discussion with Adrian who, of course, left half a forest of unwanted paperwork that I lobbed into the trash. He wandered off down the corridor to find his next best friend. Then, suddenly, I remembered that he might be able to provide funding for a European conference, so quickly shedding my ethics and judgment, I caught up with him to ask if he might provide financial support. He agreed to write a letter on my behalf requesting funding. I wore my hypocrisy with great pride.

# 23

# MALFEASANCE

## OCTOBER 26, 2004

With him, Danny had brought the usual entourage when a management team smelled medical blood. I noticed one of them eyeing my branded ballpoint pen and sandwich wrapper and half expected a corruption investigation to urgently commence. Clipboards were trembling in anticipation. I shoved the pen and wrapper into the trash to join the rest of the pharma spam.

The management posse included Danny's junior administrator, who clutched a special clipboard festooned with a Britney Spears sticker, and the manager of human resources, Tina Bowes. Bringing an HR manager was always an ominous sign because it meant there were manoeuvres afoot to suspend a doctor. Our HR manager wasn't the crisp professional one might picture. She looked as if she'd be better placed sitting in a hot dog stand at a fun fair. The woman wore a tight-fitting faux leopard nylon top with sleeves pulled up to the elbows, the better to reveal the life advice tattooed on her forearms, including REACH FOR THE STARS with two hand-drawn stars next to it. Her nails were painted a glittery purple and shaped into long talons. A forty-a-day smoking habit had left her with the deepest voice in the room. Indeed, for a moment, I thought Barry White had entered my office.

"I'm glad you agreed to help," Tina started. "I'll get straight to the point. We've been hearing a few stories about Professor Leech's unprofessional behaviour. We're now conducting a formal investigation."

I raised an eyebrow. "Unprofessional?"

"Probably *negligent* is a better word, if what I hear is correct."

"I'm not sure that it falls to a hospital HR team to define medical negligence," I countered.

The junior manager wrote all of this down, so did the HR manager as she spoke.

We were less than a minute in and the tone of the meeting was already antagonistic. "I think we need to focus on some specific complaints and maybe go from there," I suggested. I'd already taken the opportunity to personally review four of the cases that had been raised.

Previously, I'd warned Danny we had to be careful not to jump on the bandwagon because there might well be other explanations for cases in which patients had outcomes less positive than expected.

"Top of our list is removing the wrong kidney," Danny barged in. "That's known as a Never Event. In other words, it should never happen," he added unnecessarily.

I agreed this was a grave situation but was it negligent? I guessed that went without saying. But if so, whose negligence? Or was it just a terrible series of events? And were those different things?

Particularly puzzling to me was that there must have been several people in the operating room when the wrong kidney was removed, and that sometimes medical accidents happened for multiple reasons.

"The junior doctor on the wards should have marked the side of the surgery with a pen," I ventured. "Did they mark the right or wrong side?"

"There's no comment about that in the report," replied Danny.

"There were six people in the room when the procedure started," I said. "Did any of them comment when the incision was made?"

"I'm not clear about that, either," Danny told me.

"Let's go through the consent form and the notes from the admission," I suggested.

The consent form mentioned the right kidney, the one that was removed. The consent had been carried out by the junior doctor on the ward who had indeed marked the patient incorrectly, meaning he'd correctly marked the incorrect right side. The patient had consented to having his right, meaning the wrong, kidney removed.

We talked around this case, which raised more questions than answers. Was this enough to suspend Sir Desmond from work, given that the mitigating factors were quite clear? This was way outside my experience, but clearly, he whose motto was "Nothing Heals Like Cold Steel" was ultimately the person responsible. Human error in medicine was endemic.

Doctors couldn't pretend they didn't remove the wrong kidney. It was a tough one to wriggle out of. But the managers sniffed blood in the water, and since this would clearly become a civil case against the hospital, it had to be thoroughly investigated.

We worked through a few more questions, but I felt less clear about medical mistakes than I had an hour earlier.

"Should we suspend him?" asked Danny.

"Or should we improve our operating checklists," I countered. "Let's talk about another case and see if there's a pattern."

There was no pattern. The next complaint came from a young female junior doctor who claimed Leech had made a suggestive comment to her.

"What did he say?" I asked.

"He said if he was forty years younger, he'd take her back to his place."

"I expect he meant for dinner?"

"Not clear, but she was quite upset."

"Upset because she was unable to shag the professor or that he'd said this to her?" I tried to clarify. "Strange that she waited four months and only reported it when she didn't get a place on his team."

I watched the pens pausing before resuming to record the conversation. This wasn't going well.

Nurses had always been trained to report dispensing and other errors. I noted that whenever they did, the outcome was severe, and I was surprised, given the culture, that anybody would raise a hand to confess any sort of error.

If one were going to face a room full of vengeful managers, it would perhaps be preferable to say nothing when a near miss was made. If one could get away with it, one wouldn't be in any rush to report the mistake. If no harm was done, why open a whole can of worms with all the ensuing investigations and paperwork when the mistake could be learned from it and nobody would be any wiser? That was certainly the way many people felt. I sat there thinking of bad decisions I'd made, usually after eight hours awake in the middle of the night.

I recalled a fellow doctor telling me that he and his junior colleague, when they were trainees, had injected the shoulders and knees of six patients with a depo contraceptive instead of cortisone. The drugs had almost the same name and almost identical packaging. The doctor taking the drug out of the cupboard had only been in the country for two weeks. The error only came to light when the pharmacist asked why so many vials of depo contraceptive were missing from the cupboard — not usually considered a high-risk drug for theft. Apparently, the two doctors both felt the need to remain quiet. None of the patients came to any harm and eventually improved, and none became pregnant, either, I suspected.

We achieved little in the meeting. Tina agreed to formally list the concerns, and for now at least, the Leech was able to continue to practise.

I needed to pop up to Ward 3 to review a patient who had had a bone-marrow biopsy earlier in the day. No sooner had I strode into the nurses' office than I was assailed by two staff nurses asking me if I'd like to make a donation to Ali's leaving present.

"Who's Ali?" I asked.

They both laughed.

"You're the funniest, Dr. Standish," said one of them. "I think Alison's been here longer than anybody."

I smiled as if I'd been joking all along. One of them handed me a large card about eight by twelve inches full of witty quips from colleagues. They encouraged me to write in it.

"Most people are putting £20 in the pot," said Staff Nurse No. 1, who I could see from a badge was called Deborah. I was about to very grudgingly agree to shed more of my hard-earned cash when the other one, who now had a name, Heidi, added, "But most of the consultant staff have donated £50."

That was a huge amount of money by any standard. Literally, I felt that every step I took, people robbed me. I had to develop a new strategy. Perhaps lying and pretending I was a regular donor to a specific charity and that I wanted to limit my giving to that one cause would do the trick.

I walked up a floor to another ward where I was again assaulted. This time I was asked to contribute to a birthday present for Nina. I was wise to the scam by now and didn't ask how much she wanted but simply reached into my wallet and pulled out the only £5 note I had there. Handing it over with a smile, I said, "This is all I have. I hope it helps."

"Of course," I was told. "That's very generous, I'll put the money toward getting Nina groomed."

As it turned out, Nina was her pet poodle.

On my way home, I dropped into the supermarket. Catherine had asked me to buy some oven chips. I used my initiative and also bought a frozen curry dish from the same freezer.

When I got to the checkout and was about to pay, the cashier asked me if I'd like to donate £2 for the children's hospice. I braced myself, having practised this in the car. All I needed to say was "No, thank you. I already have a charity of choice I donate to."

"No, thank you," I said bravely.

I swore all of the conveyor belts stopped and every customer in the supermarket glanced my way. A hush fell over the whole place. The cashier glared at me as if I hated all children and wanted them to die of cancer. Behind me, a child of about four stared at me silently.

"Because I'd rather donate £10 if I may," I blurted.

Thankfully, everybody in the queue heard that, and I was fairly sure a couple of people recognized me. I'd always believed giving to charity was a little bit of a waste of time unless other people knew what you'd done, though you never had to overtly tell anybody. Better to be caught humbly giving.

A few minutes later, I was about to pull into the driveway of my house but saw Inspector McAlister's car there. I parked a few hundred yards up the road and called Catherine to tell her I was at a meeting, and within five minutes, the front door opened and McAlister strode to his car. Only a few moments later, I was home and in the house.

Catherine was crying. The body had been identified. "They say it was Therese Headley," she sobbed. "I can't believe Richard actually went ahead and killed her. Apparently, they haven't even arrested him yet. They want to talk to you, too."

My mind instantly returned to the incriminating beer mat. What had I done with it that day? Had I left it? I had no recollection.

This was the year that chocolate-covered coffee beans suddenly became *de rigueur* — a ridiculous idea, since the outcome with hindsight was obvious. There was a little bowl of them in the kitchen, so I grabbed one, and mere seconds later, cracked a tooth. This was the depressing slide into middle age. I'd begun to realize the effects of physical decline in a bookshop when browsing the latest bestsellers, commenting to Catherine about the small type font. Two weeks later, I was wearing my first bifocals. What would be next? Heart disease? Grey pubes?

The phone rang several times that evening. Each call was another friend of Catherine's calling to know if she'd heard about the identity of the body. I honestly felt this was the most excitement some of them had had for a long time, such was their eagerness to spread the terrible news.

Over the phone, Catherine said, "I gather the older body was just a pile of bones, but they think it might be that girl who went missing in 1987."

It was probably best not to tell her that the body was distinctly male. The more alarming thought occurred to me that despite the skeleton being in the Kilminster pathology department for several days, not a single person had spotted the metal band running from the mandible to the base of the skull each side to keep the two together. Our pathologist had clearly moved from mediocre to weak.

The next day, I awoke with zero enthusiasm for work but managed to drag myself in, only to discover another in-patient referral request up on the surgical ward. It was just before eight o'clock, which should be a good time to catch the patient. I saw Leech making his way around his post-operative patients.

He went up to a Mr. Blaney whom I'd been asked to consult on and peeled back the dressing on the man's wound. A bead of pus emerged from the suture line. When the professor pressed on the edges, more pus leaked out.

"This looks fine," Leech said.

He moved on to the next patient without washing his hands and shook her hands warmly. The ward round continued in this fashion with no handwashing. The Methicillin-resistant Staphylococcus aureus, better known as MRSA, from the first patient gradually spread around the ward. Nobody made a comment. To be fair, the wash basin on the bay was unusable because, oddly, a bedpan had been put in it. The odder thing was that it had been there for two days.

The next patient on Sir Demond's rounds had just arrived on the ward. She was due to have a laparoscopic cholecystectomy. In other words, her gallbladder would be removed with minimally invasive surgery using three small cuts in the abdomen.

As I was to learn, three hours later, having cleaned the area for surgery and draped the patient with green sheets, the professor asked for a scalpel, which was handed to him by Sally, the scrub nurse.

"Thank you, Ruby," Leech said. He then proceeded to cut a seven-inch incision in the upper-right abdominal wall.

"I thought this was a laparoscopic procedure," said the anesthetist.

"Nonsense. You carry on being a gas man and leave the rest to me. As I've said time and time again, *nothing heals like cold steel.* The bigger the incision the safer the procedure because I can see everything I need to see."

Nobody else in the operating room said a word, and the surgical assistant, his trainee, carried on with the open cholecystectomy. Halfway through the procedure, Leech suddenly announced he was going to leave the rest to his assistant, promptly tore off his gloves, and left the room.

When I got home after a very long day, Catherine appeared triumphant as I walked through the door and stepped over three industrial black bags.

"I've had the best day," she said to me. "I've been clearing the wardrobes. Look! Three whole bags of clothes for you to take to the charity shop."

I'd always believed Catherine had too many clothes and shoes, so this was excellent news. Half of what she bought she wore once, and I never saw it again. "I bet you've made loads of space in your wardrobe."

"Well, not exactly," she replied with a big smile. "I haven't got to my side yet. These are all your clothes."

No sense of the irony that I was already limited to twenty percent of the wardrobe space.

# 24

# Blood Clot

## October 28, 2004

On Thursday, I hobbled into work. I had a numb left calf and low back pain. The previous afternoon, I'd been flattened by a four-hundred-pound sack of potatoes. I'd been listening to the heart of a patient who was sitting with her legs hanging off the side of the examination table. When I completed that, I glanced up and noticed she was staring vacantly at me, face pale, having mysteriously fainted. Gracefully, she started to topple forward, and for a naive moment, I thought I could guide her to a prone position on the bed. Seconds later, she was lying on top of me on the floor, my left leg bent underneath me and my back already asking why I'd tried to lift twice my body weight.

I was trapped there for about fifteen seconds, at which point her eyes opened, her face about an inch from my own. Somehow I was able to roll her off and struggle to my feet. She was uninjured, having had a softer landing than I did.

It was only a few days since I'd fallen off the stepladder while performing my well-intentioned sabotage of Morris's extension plans. So much had happened since then.

I had to see another patient that morning on the surgical ward. She'd had a post-operative blood clot, a thrombosis, which had then travelled up to the lung — a pulmonary embolism. I limped to the nurses' office where I sat reviewing the patient notes and chatting to Vanessa, one of the nurses. Halfway through the conversation, her phone pinged.

"Oh, my God, I'm ovulating!" she cried out.

I was a little taken aback, all the more so when she told me she now needed intense sex for the next two days because her cervical mucus was in a state of perfect viscosity.

People shared far too much nowadays. It wasn't helped by the fact that I knew her husband, a two-hundred-and-eighty-five-pound ginger-bearded man of about five foot five. One hundred and seventy-five pounds of his weight sat in his beer belly, and try as I might, I couldn't stop thinking about the mechanics of their sexual act. A little bit of sick came up into my mouth as she told me that this might be one of many children he'd had, since he'd been a sperm donor for several years until he was told he no longer represented the type of man most women would choose to be the virtual father of their child.

"I'm not off till four. I may have to call him to come in during my break," she told me.

Next, she'd ask if he could use my office.

Then I noticed Professor Leech with his entourage in the same bay as my patient. He was wearing his old school tie, his usual choice when a bow tie wasn't immediately available. He'd spilled food on the tie and wasn't quite the immaculate dresser colleagues described him as.

Leech's junior doctors were either shrinking into the background looking terrified or pushing themselves into his field of view in a desperate attempt to get their tongues as far up his rectum as the sigmoidoscope he wielded in clinic. Few things were more nauseating than to see a grovelling junior doctor, particularly an Oxford graduate who possessed fifteen percent more ability to bootlick than a graduate from any other medical school laughing at a second-rate joke.

"Where's the gallbladder?" asked Sir Desmond petulantly. One of the Oxford graduates excitedly answered, describing the exact anatomical position of the organ.

Leech shushed him impatiently. What I knew he meant was: "Where's the patient, Mrs. Brown, who had her gallbladder removed yesterday?"

She was down getting an X-ray, which clearly angered the professor who, with an irritated sigh, moved on to the next bed, muttering about how this wouldn't have happened thirty years ago. The nurses hadn't shared with Leech the impending complaint that the laparoscopic keyhole surgery had been abandoned for the more invasive procedure.

The patient I was to see also wasn't there but would be back soon, the nurses told me. She was a forty-eight-year-old, heavy-smoking diabetic recovering from a partial colectomy that had been complicated by an MRSA wound infection. To me, she had plenty of reasons to get a blood clot post-operatively. Obviously, though, she didn't see the irony in the fact that even after having such a complication she still travelled down to the hospital entrance for her next cigarette and stood under a NO SMOKING sign, all the while dragging her intravenous fluids hanging from a pole on a wheeled base. As often as not, she'd trudge through the entrance hall with the back of her hospital gown partially open, already extracting a cigarette from a packet cleverly disguised in a small leather pouch. A second pouch hung around her neck on a leather thong and held her lighter.

I returned to the nurses' office and chatted with Vanessa, the ovulating staff nurse, as I waited for my patient. Vanessa mentioned that lately things weren't so good on the ward. Many patients were complaining about more post-operative pain than was usually the case, and it was clear she believed this was related to the surgeon involved, which happened to be Sir Desmond. I wondered if there was a bandwagon effect at play, with everyone beginning to blame him for anything that didn't go to plan. I checked the patient notes and quickly ascertained that Leech hadn't even performed this particular procedure! One of his trainees had done it.

As we sat there talking, Vanessa's male nursing colleague, Robert Turney, came in. He was a slightly unkempt fellow in his early thirties, had a pale, sweaty appearance, and always needed a shave. Apparently, this scrofulous aspect was all the rage, though I'd had him assist in my clinic a few years earlier when he'd seemed distinctly better presented. Rob was the person I'd seen hanging around outside the Silver Cod in a hoodie, the badge of most criminals, I mused.

Even Sir Desmond had lately developed the unshaven look. Momentarily, I reflected that perhaps I, too, should grow a little facial hair. The professor could even deliver a bon mot occasionally. One time, a social worker had approached him and asked if she could discuss the "client" in bed twelve.

"Client?" he exclaimed. "Client? Prostitutes have clients. I have patients."

Robert was due to finish his shift soon, but because the ward was chronically understaffed, he kindly volunteered to stay an extra hour and do the afternoon drug round, which consisted mainly of giving routine post-operative antibiotics, analgesia, and, of course, the medication the patients had been taking before they came in for their surgery. Perhaps I'd misjudged him.

He asked me about a mutual patient he recalled from when we'd worked together. I was about to reply when Sir Desmond and his team strolled into the room, oblivious to those already there. The surgical team all sat down and started chattering loudly, which was a good moment for me to leave. Sadly, despite waiting for twenty minutes, my patient's smoking habit and her ability to natter incessantly to fellow addicts had conspired against us meeting that day.

I called Catherine, who was off work. It was one of those special days teachers had to prevent exhaustion from setting in. Since I was leaving the hospital earlier than usual, she suggested I meet her halfway home at the supermarket. I'd walked into this situation and was caught in the classical unwinnable state of affairs described by Brian's Shopping Theorem: "In any partnership, there should only be one primary grocery shopper. Subsidiary shoppers complicate the process. The primary shopper has the right to complain about all outcomes."

For a number of weeks, Catherine had expressed subtle but inarguable discontent about my lack of engagement in the grocery-shopping needs of our household. To the more enlightened, this was an entirely reasonable stance. After all, in any relationship, why shouldn't there be a clear sharing of the chores?

The challenge was that if shopping were a Venn diagram, the overlap of chosen products as we toured the shop was surprisingly small. Inevitably, there were two options. Either purchase all products, or the primary shopper could exercise her power of veto. It just happened that in our relationship the power of veto was considerable and didn't lie with me.

And so it was, as I returned items to the shelf, I felt slightly sad we would have no popcorn for that evening but triumphant that I wouldn't be invited to perform a combined shopping trip for at least three months.

# 25

# The Wedding

## October 30, 2004

Spider and Sunshine were to pledge their troth today, and we'd packed the car ready for the eighty-mile journey to the wedding. I was glad to pull out of our driveway. The police were still at the Furniss residence. I could just make out not one but three of the white tents the police use at crime scenes. Cars had been coming and going for days. Morris and his wife, Maggy, had returned from their cruise the night before, expecting to see a half-built extension and instead facing a series of interviews from the police.

Harvey had asked if he could stay in our house this weekend to look after the children and dog, which suited us fine. He'd already found himself a vantage point in the upstairs spare bedroom to watch events unfold.

Planning for the wedding day hadn't gone particularly well. We'd arranged, a few days earlier, to meet Catherine's sister, along with Sunshine and Spider and Sunshine's younger brother, Raymond, at a restaurant in town. Spider was a no-show. Presumably, he was still in the pub with his friends, or if Sunshine were lucky, perhaps, he'd fallen into the canal, which I calculated would still save me a considerable amount of money and salvage what was predicted by me to be a dreadful weekend. Tasks were allotted for the coming celebration.

I'd forgotten to book a hotel, so we were staying in a bed and breakfast close to the Rugby Club. When I packed the car, I didn't forget the wedding present, but not the Wedgwood dinner set the couple had requested. Catherine and I had a standoff over the gift, since my position was that Spider and Sunshine were utterly uncultured and probably rarely used a plate. In the end, we agreed a deep-fat fryer was more appropriate, since their vitamin-depleted appearance suggested that was their main method of cooking.

We were supposed to arrive by 10:00 a.m. in order to collect the barbecue from Spider's and drop it off outside the kitchen of the Rugby Club, so we made an early start. Catherine's sister was delegated to collect the meat first thing that morning and put it in the fridge, then she and Catherine would decorate the Club Hall. The timeline was fairly tight. My second mission was to collect the flowers for each table, along with a bunch of blooms for the bride to carry up the aisle. Somebody had forgotten to order these, and both florists in town were unable to help at the last minute, but we were assured that if I got to Tesco's Superstore before noon, it would have everything we needed.

Earlier, we'd arranged to drop our bags off at our accommodation. The bed and breakfast wasn't quite what we'd expected. Our bedroom was relatively compact, and there was a shared bathroom down the corridor currently occupied by another guest whom I suspected had amoebic dysentery, judging by the noise. Catherine always preferred a high-end hotel with high-thread-count sheets and pillows that didn't smell of sweaty heads, chip oil, and garam masala. What we had was light blue nylon sheets that had gone out of style in the 1970s. Catherine then foolishly peeled back the pillowcase to reveal a yellow pillow stained with the slobber of a thousand guests.

Suffice to say, this was potentially going to be another test of our relationship, and already I was getting the sense things were extremely tenuous. I called around to a few hotels for something more in keeping with what God had intended for Catherine but had no luck — even considered driving us home again that evening and offered to make the ultimate sacrifice of avoiding the gooseberry wine. Catherine, meanwhile, placed a towel over the pillows and sent me off to the shops to buy a different bath towel, along with some bath cleaner and a cloth, since she was confident the bathroom wouldn't pass muster, either.

I set off on my errands, starting with the towels, then moved on to Spider's to get the barbecue. What I hadn't realized was that there was no trailer, and I was expected to manoeuvre the barbecue into the back of our car. Spider wasn't home, having already headed to the pub with his friends for a final drink before the wedding, which was scheduled for 2:00 p.m. So, his mother made a desultory effort to help me. Luckily, since it was relatively small, we were able to wrestle the contraption into the car.

Then I drove to the Rugby Club to discover that the artificial coals in the barbecue had all spilled out, along with about a pint of rancid three-year-old fat and oil that had soaked into the new towels I'd bought an hour earlier. Dragging the barbecue out, I replaced the coals, wiped my hands on the new towels, returned to buy a second set of towels, and went back to the bed and breakfast, having accomplished the mission.

Catherine seemed a little discontented. She'd drawn the curtains in our bedroom and discovered a stain on the bottom of the curtain that looked as if it might glow in black light. I went to clean the bathtub for her. There was the scum from a thousand bodies that proved stubborn to remove but could be disguised by bubbles if I added enough of the bubble bath I'd bought at Tesco, hoping this would herald a new calm in the day. Sadly, the water was tepid, and upon lying in it, Catherine discovered not one but three pubic hairs, while at the same time being afforded a view of the toilet rim, confirming that the cleaner had taken a relaxed approach to its task.

Next, I left to do the flower run. It was unclear to me why so many key roles landed on our shoulders and all on the morning of the wedding. As I drove to Tesco to buy the flowers, it dawned on me that the chance of recouping the money I'd spent on them was about zero. The mission was a small bouquet for the bride to hold, five white carnations or roses for Spider and his grooms, and fourteen small bunches of flowers for the table decorations.

Tesco had some wilting chrysanthemums but no roses or carnations. I bought what I could: fourteen potted houseplants for the tabletops. On the way back, I was filling up the car with fuel and noticed some additional flowers in a bucket by the pumps, so I purchased two more bunches, knowing we could split these up for the groomsmen.

Who could have predicted the combination of pitiful disdain and disapproval that greeted me when I arrived with my bounty? But as a seasoned husband, it was water off a duck's back. Admittedly, some of the flowers were a little brown around the petals, but after I received a rather unnecessary barbed quip from Catherine, I fully realized Sunshine couldn't carry a potted hyacinth up the aisle.

The Rugby Club bar was now a wedding reception venue, though it still looked very much like a rugby club bar. Spider's friend, known as Grunt, was setting up a turntable he'd recently acquired and appeared mysteriously to know little about how the equipment was put together.

The meat was in the fridge, and I was given the job of cutting up thirty baguettes. We were ahead of time. It was only 1:30 p.m. Nothing could go wrong.

We arrived at the church where a couple of gardeners were smoking at the entrance. Politely, I asked them to leave when the guests arrived, only to learn they were Spider's ushers.

The bride and groom walked up the aisle to Adele's "Rolling in the Deep." Apparently, they had asked for "Make You Feel My Love," but the organist had downloaded the wrong sheet music. We learned that Adele didn't always translate to church organ successfully.

All I recalled from the actual service was feeling intensely irritated by a set of red-haired twins of about seven running amok in the church. One of them, I was sure, was the same child I'd accidentally tripped up in a ballpark two years earlier when he kept dashing around me. I gave the creature one of my dark stares.

Equally irritated was Catherine — not with the twins but with me. For reasons I didn't fully understand, the only time I got a frog in my throat was at the theatre or weddings. No sooner had the vicar started to talk than I developed the worst tickle in my throat, which I quietly cleared. A few seconds later, I tried again. This did nothing to alleviate the situation, so I decided to get things over and done with by performing one loud cough that coincided with the vicar asking the congregation to "Speak now or forever hold your peace."

About eighty faces turned to stare at me, including Spider, who for a moment appeared panicked, leading me to suspect that perhaps there might be an underlying concern that needed to be voiced. I got a death glare from Catherine. But it was necessary for me to cough, so I had.

Before we knew it, the service was over and they were rushing out to Kylie Minogue singing "The Locomotion," another error. We returned to the Club House where Edith, who was in charge of the main course — barbecued ribs — was in a state of almost complete meltdown because there was no gas cylinder for the barbecue.

Catherine's expression made it clear this was entirely my fault, so she sent me off urgently back to the bed and breakfast to pick up the car and drive around aimlessly in a town I'd never been to before to find a gas cylinder. Luckily, I finally located one in the do-it-yourself store on the outskirts of town. I should have gone there first instead of discovering it forty minutes later.

Interestingly, the person who sold me the cylinder was a ginger-haired man of about thirty. I wondered if he might be the mysterious donor responsible for the plague of children who were eroding my quality of life. Every red-headed male I saw looked like a potential sperm donor to me. For a moment, I imagined him in a small room making the donation, thus causing me reluctantly to lift the gas cylinder after he took it out of a large outdoor cage.

I returned to a surprisingly happy reception where the melon balls had been consumed, the bread was eaten, and most of the tables were on their second or third bottle of elderflower wine. There were at least four ghastly children running around, one of whom was yet another seven-year-old red-headed thing who kept knocking into my table. When I gave him one of my impatient looks, his mother proudly told me he had attention deficit hyperactive disorder, which I suspect in this case meant he was a badly behaved normal child.

Admittedly, the ribs took more than ninety minutes for Edith to cook because the barbecue was a compact one, but nobody seemed to mind, and Grunt had already started the music when Catherine and I crept out, having filled out the wedding guest book.

Catherine wrote: "Beautiful couple, best wishes for the future."

I wrote: "I'll give it six months," which turned out to be correct.

The following morning, we arose a little stiff and jaded. The man in the next room had chatted until about two in the morning, but owing to his somewhat startling appearance, a cross between cage fighter and high-security prison inmate, we'd let him talk. Besides, the nylon sheets had a life of their own and kept sliding off the mattress, which itself was the equivalent of a wafer. Catherine very graciously omitted to blame me for the choice of accommodation, even when her toast arrived and could be folded into four and unfolded while preserving its elasticity.

We drove home. As I unpacked the car, I realized the deep-fat fryer, our gift for the newlyweds, was still there. I elected to say nothing and took it to the shed. Even a month later when Catherine moaned about the lack of a thank-you letter, I kept my counsel. I was a survivor.

Arriving home, late morning on the Sunday, we noticed immediately that the police remained at the Furniss residence.

I was sick with anxiety. Planting the old bones had seemed a relatively harmless strategy, but it had already occupied the police for several days. It was essential that I never confess to having had any part in the plan. I suspected Catherine could clearly see straight through my feeble act of confusion about what could possibly be going on.

I saw Inspector McAlister spot us and stride in our direction, and I tried to nonchalantly head into the house but was too late. In his slightly scary Glaswegian accent, he pronounced, "Dr. Standish, you're back. Why is it that every time I find a body, you're somehow involved?"

"Involved?" I replied. "I've literally just got home." I could sense guilt written all over my face and was waiting for the cuffs to be slapped on.

"Can I come in? I need to ask you a few questions?"

Catherine welcomed him in enthusiastically, offering him a coffee.

"Well, it's way past *beer* o'clock," said McAlister. "Have you got anything stronger?"

Catherine went to fetch him a can of Heineken.

In the end, it was a gentle questioning rather than a Stasi interrogation. Had I seen anything unusual at the Furniss residence in the past few days? I affected the most guileless face I could manage and claimed to have seen absolutely nothing. He held my gaze a little too long.

I had the choice of blurting out that I might have accidently dropped an ancient skeleton into the footings of the extension, or … Instead, I suddenly burst out with "Milky Norm who lives over the Silver Cod did tell me his mother had gone missing. Do you think she's the body you found?" I'm not sure why I said this, knowing it was already well established that Therese Headley was the victim.

The inspector smiled slightly. "No, I know exactly who she is. And so does most of Kilminster, but not apparently you. And I *do* know you're tied up in this murder because I saw you and Dr. Headley planning it in the Green Dragon." He held up a small plastic bag containing a beer mat with my writing on it.

Before the blood had even halfway drained from my face, McAlister rose to leave.

# 26

# The Cruise

## November 1, 2004

I was saved from immediate arrest by Catherine having booked us on a five-day-long Caribbean cruise to celebrate our fifteenth wedding anniversary. Nobody wanted to go on a cruise in November because it was the tail end of hurricane season, which was why we could afford it.

Harvey was going to stay on at our house to take care of the children. I could think of few things worse than being cooped up on a ship with a group of human beings I hadn't chosen and of whom a few would be the ones who spread norovirus diarrhea around the whole boat. I imagined overweight, snaggle-toothed, tattooed women from a mining town in northern England accompanied by their partners with earrings and mullets troughing their way through the buffet and avoiding anything that wasn't deep-fried.

"They aren't all like that," insisted Catherine. "There are lots of people like us."

That was hardly a resounding recommendation. I pictured Catherine's friend, Emma Blenkinsop, and her husband, David, whom she described as people like us even though they sang songs from West End musicals in harmony and knew most of the words to *The Sound of Music* and *Oliver!* I'd find myself stuck with middle-class families discussing school fees and suffer general knowledge quizzes at 5:00

p.m. in which the same family won each day. Perhaps even worse, I pictured street vendors selling cheap sunglasses and cork necklaces or wrapping a friendship bracelet around Catherine's wrist so that I felt forced to pay for it. Worst of all, though, would be the pool deck, which I considered a compelling argument against democracy.

"How do you know you won't like them?" asked Catherine.

"Because there are few human beings on this planet I can bear to be near," I shot back.

Surely by now Catherine had an inkling that I didn't care to be in the company of my fellow humans.

But there we were on a cruise of the Caribbean, starting in Miami, which as a city was about as appealing as a bad case of herpes. We'd flown in from Gatwick Airport to join the ship at 4:00 p.m. By that time, my wallet was stolen at gunpoint and I'd spent two hours on the phone to the bank trying to cancel my credit cards. That was the second time I'd been robbed when travelling.

Day Two was called the "Day at Sea," which essentially meant bobbing around the ocean doing about two knots to save the cruise company the cost of docking somewhere. It also encouraged passengers to spend money on things they didn't need, such as jewellery, watches, and silk scarves.

I decided to visit the spa and paid an exorbitant amount of cash for a hot-stone massage. My therapist, Molly, lived in Swaffham in a two-bedroom semi-detached house. It had an open-plan kitchen-living area with grey cabinets and a new sofa from Ikea. She had a little cockapoo called Rachel, which slept on her bed. The sheets were also from Ikea, and her mother had made her a quilt.

How did I know all that? Because she didn't stop talking from the moment I was lying face down peering through a small hole until fifteen minutes in when her recent chest infection got the better of her. I distinctly felt a lump of phlegm land on my lower back as she coughed her lungs up before resuming the description of her life. She moved on to her cute little car, an orange Volkswagen Beetle called Miranda, and then out of the blue she placed a red-hot stone the size of a baked potato on my back.

Forty-five minutes later, I expected to be relaxing in the spa quiet area reading a book. Instead, I was irritable, in pain, and £100 worse off. Before I could limp back to my cabin — known by the cruise company as a stateroom, to add a touch of grandeur to the trip — Molly returned holding two boxes with turquoise ribbons.

"This is the Paraguayan Seaweed Serum," she explained. "And this is the Essential Oil Cassava Complex, which will remove toxins from your body."

Suddenly, I felt a great deal better. Nothing beat an unexpected free gift. I thanked her profusely, and she placed them in an expensive paper bag with the spa logo on the front, stuffing the spare space with blue tissue.

"You can pay for these at the front as you leave," she added, somewhat deflating me, but nowhere near as much as when I swiped my cruise card and discovered these two bogus products were going to cost me another £200, not to mention the compulsory twenty percent gratuity.

"This is a tax, not a tip," I said to the little Filipina girl on reception. She just smiled, and I lost all will to fight it.

On Day Three of the cruise, I made the mistake of passing the sundeck on my hunt for a quiet corner where I could read. Try to imagine two hundred white bodies, each at least fifty pounds overweight, metamorphosizing into two hundred scarlet bodies over eight hours.

Catherine suggested, on Day Four, that we walk up into the town for lunch on the small island we were currently docked at. Most places seemed too expensive to me, but I found a rustic, cheap-looking place tucked away up a side street. A stray dog was peeing against the doorway as we approached, but there were no other signs of trouble ahead, though I could tell Catherine believed I was becoming ever more miserly and not embracing the spirit of the vacation. We ordered our food from a surly Greek who glared at me as if he preferred I'd never left home. On that we agreed.

The chef, possibly, might have died and been replaced by a passing child. To say my food was disappointing was to ignore the public health crisis demonstrated by the cooking. The cuttlefish had died of old age and reminded me of a uterus that had just been removed and was on its way to the pathology lab.

Meanwhile, Catherine's swordfish was actually a carp recently plucked from a back garden fish pond. The potatoes had been cooked five days earlier and partially warmed up. The side salad had already featured on four previous diners' plates.

Catherine gave me a look that said, "We should leave now, you cheap bastard, whom I never should have married."

She didn't need to say anything. I left $50, and we escaped up the alley while the owner was in the kitchen presumably examining the roadkill he'd gathered that day for tonight's dinner.

It was a relief to get back to the damp drizzle of Gatwick Airport and cross cruising off my list of life experiences. I was looking forward to getting back to work; Catherine was strangely quiet on the way home, almost as if I was difficult to live with.

We arrived at our house late in the evening, but Harvey, as was becoming a habit, was at the door with an excited look on his face. "They're going to arrest Richard Headley for killing Therese. The woman in the post office told me he smashed her skull in with a hammer. They're still looking for the weapon. As for the skeleton, they still have no idea who it is yet."

For about six seconds, no words were spoken.

Catherine stared at me. "Wait! Skeleton? Brian, please tell me I'm wrong."

"Wrong about what?" I asked, no doubt appearing guilty as sin, all the while darting a flash of anger at my brother.

Harvey caught my expression and attempted, unsuccessfully I suspected, to backtrack and claim little knowledge of the goings-on two doors up the road.

"Don't you have a skeleton in the attic?" demanded Catherine.

"No, I got rid of that years ago," I lied, then remembering the suitcase in which the bones had been kept would have been close to the black balaclava.

"You know something, Brian," accused Catherine.

"Actually, it was me," said Harvey in a rare moment of filial loyalty.

We went inside and confessed everything. The only lie being that Harvey took full responsibility for burying the skeleton while I agreed with him that I knew nothing about it. The three of us made a pact never to discuss the skeleton again.

# 27

# THE LAST SUPPER

## NOVEMBER 12, 2004

The following Friday, we were invited out, and I did my best to find a plausible reason to decline the commitment.

Mark Stone, a local family doctor, had called to invite us to a dining club he was setting up. Essentially, there would be six couples, each in turn entertaining the others every two months. The rules included a defined limited budget to avoid fiscal competition and no bottle of wine was allowed a date, thus limiting it to the cheapest available. Mark graciously hosted the first event.

I wasn't sure why he asked us to go, since I'd always done my best to avoid his company. Indeed, I mentioned my dislike of Stone to my friend, Warwick Tetlow, one of the other guests, when we first arrived at Mark's.

"Blowing out Mark's candle doesn't make yours shine any brighter," he pronounced piously.

I felt like a terrible human being. What had I become slagging my host?

"Mind you," continued Warwick, "I agree. He's a total a-hole. Definitely needs a bullet."

I felt a little better.

Even before we ate, the group divided along chromosomal lines, with the women apparently having a better time. This was a disappointment to me because every male at the event seemed to own some sort of little red racing car and spent the first hour talking about where an original chrome bumper for a TR6 might be sourced. I assumed they were talking about a car. Then they switched to rugby as a topic. Apparently, there was some sort of international competition that real men enthusiastically conjectured about. I would have preferred to tell them about my new DEWALT compound mitre saw, so I sidled along the hallway to be with the ladies. I was just outside the kitchen where they were gathered.

The women were choosing some of their favourite films from the 1970s and 1980s for a film club they'd decided to create. Catherine's friend from work, Rianne Kyle, suggested they watch *10* with Dudley Moore and Bo Derek. I went back to the other room to grab my beer and returned just as Catherine was telling Alison she'd only ever heard the first two minutes of *Boléro*, which caused great amusement between them but meant nothing to me.

The meal was tuna-and-sweetcorn pasta, a staple of students up and down the land. It was slightly spoiled by Mark's version of a Caesar salad, which was mainly three browning, wilted pieces of lettuce decorated with burnt toast cubes and a decorative swirl of what might have been Mark's ejaculate. Over the meal, the couples tried to get to know one another. I'd met most of them, but there was a new obstetrician and gynecologist at the hospital, William Handy. Catherine asked why he'd chosen to become a gynecologist.

"Because I get severe Raynaud's" was his answer, which thankfully was totally lost on most of the Economy Dining Club, so nobody pursued it.

Personally, I wouldn't have been attracted to a job where I could expect to see two hundred vaginas per week in various states of disrepair for forty years. I noticed he was wearing a little lapel pin with an *M* on it. I asked what it was.

"I'm a member of Mensa," he answered smugly.

I knew that *menses* was probably Latin for "menstruation," so I assumed *mensa* was some sort of association for people interested in women's periods.

"As a hematologist, I'm not sure I'd be granted entry," I replied.

He agreed and we moved on.

And then it happened, of course. Inspired by the presence of a gynecologist, the female guests began to overshare about their challenges downstairs. From that moment on, I couldn't help imagining Tim Skinner's ex-wife Emily, who had returned to her maiden name, Harrison, and whose gusset was getting ever damper every time she laughed after she gladly shared her life of stress incontinence, apparently leaking with every sneeze. I remembered something from school about rats not having a bladder, and now I'd always imagine Emily, like a rat, leaving a steady, light flow of urine.

Any female who had a child seemed compelled to perform the birth auction, wherein the aim was to outbid the previous person with an ever more dire account of how close the birth came to tragedy, or how much vulval trauma it entailed. Upon reflection, I never thought an episiotomy was ever good dinnertime conversation.

One thing I was grateful about: Nigel Robinson hadn't been invited. His desperate ongoing attempts at banter and unrelenting innuendos had hit a new low at a local Continuing Professional Development evening where we had a fish dish with fingerling potatoes and he asked one of the female local family doctors if he could take a photograph of her red snapper. Then he added a touch of science by asking if anybody knew how to make a hormone.

We played a game where you had to answer questions showing how well you knew your partner. One was: "If your partner were a cocktail, what would they be?"

I tried hard to find a cocktail that encapsulated Catherine: classy, smooth, sophisticated. Before I could name one, I heard Catherine say, "Well that's easy. Brian's an old-fashioned sour."

I lost spirit at that point.

During the meal, we heard more manly stories. Mark, Tim, and Warwick were still going to the gym every Sunday evening. Inevitably, all they could talk about was the number of pounds they could lift and which protein powder they used.

I'd lasted one partial evening at the gym before realizing they were all running from their destiny and unlikely to win the race. Mark was in his late fifties, and I reminded him that once he entered his sixties he'd be in Sniper Alley. However fit he kept himself, there was a bullet with his name on it that would eventually hit home. Sooner rather than later, I thought to myself.

Mark then rattled on at me about how aerobic exercise and a Mediterranean diet would prolong his life, his oversize pectoral muscles twitching threateningly beneath his shirt, which predictably was a size too small to emphasize his chiselled perfection.

I had the last laugh, though, because it turned out I was a prophet. Five days after the inaugural Economy Dining Club meal, Mark dropped dead from a heart attack while making a high-protein smoothie. The Sniper had done a good job, and the world seemed ever so slightly to be a better place. Mark's candle was blown out for good and mine indeed started to glow a little brighter.

I didn't recall much about the funeral other than realizing the colleague providing the eulogy struggled to convince us that Mark was anything other than a conceited egomaniac. The same colleague walked off holding the newly bereaved widow's hand, heading in the direction of the Holiday Inn to offer her practical comfort.

# 28

# Organic Beef

## November 13, 2004

I was in the doghouse again. Huw Powys was one of the two dermatologists at my hospital. Even for a nationalist Welshman, he was particularly belligerent, with a jowly red face that made him look as if he'd witnessed a nuclear blast. But in an unexpected turn of kindness, he offered us the chance to buy a quarter of one of his cows, which was shortly to take a one-way journey to the abattoir to be butchered to nourish Kilminster's finest meat eaters.

A little background might be in order here. There was a tendency for some male hospital specialists to spontaneously assume they were farmers. They bought small holdings they could ill afford, started off with a couple of chickens, and evolved via a pair of goats to keeping cows. At some point, the dire economics of the situation, and the reality of the impossibility of making a profit from the hobby, became evident. Thus, inevitably, the fiscal challenge always ended up with these doctor farmers unable to pay their vile children's school fees. Most went through the following process:

> **Step 1:** Slaughter some animals to try to recoup the initial costs by selling the meat to unsuspecting colleagues.

**Step 2:** Rent out the fields to try to cover the mortgage.
**Step 3:** Sell up and move to a more sensible home.

However, the specialist at this point proceeded to **Step 4**, bypassing **Step 3**, in which, if there was a wife, they bought a horse for her. This rapidly became at least two horses, since there was always a child called Tabitha or Cordelia who "needed" a pony. Suddenly, there were saddles and reins and jodhpurs and helmets to purchase. Then there were veterinary bills simply unaffordable to anybody who wasn't involved in banking, pharma, or the other sort of drug dealing. School fees, vet bills, and saddles forced the specialist to abandon all principles, and private medicine became his only hope, along with an unscrupulous close relationship with Big Pharma.

Huw, bless his Welsh soul, was only at **Step 1** at this point. He offered me a huge amount of beef at an attractive discount. Admittedly, I didn't have a clue how much one normally paid for a joint of beef, but I readily agreed to pay £200 for the local organic grass-fed beef.

About a week later, Huw appeared in the driveway with a massive amount of meat that he off-loaded at the front door. Thankfully, Catherine was still at work, so I had time to plan. That meant I had time to call Harvey and ask him if we could use his trailer to go into town to buy a small deep freezer, since there was no other way of storing such a ridiculous amount of beef.

Off we drove to a box store on the edge of town where I purchased a small chest freezer along with a new satnav for my car and a new steam iron. I wasn't sure if we needed the last, but it was an attractive shade of deep blue and bound to score me points.

We achieved this within three hours, installing the deep freezer in the back of the garage. After I filled it with the beef, I was on the edge of one of those triumphant zeniths in a relationship.

Two hours later, Catherine arrived home, a little fractious after an encounter with a parent who objected to his child being given a B minus for some homework which, by the sound of it, the parent had completed himself. To improve her mood, I guided her first to the kitchen to present the new iron and then to the garage where I showed her the new freezer with the meat that was going to save us a fortune.

I wasn't entirely certain what the time was from the potential of a perfect moment to utter despair, but it was surprisingly short. In essence, there were two issues. The first was that I'd bought a new freezer, the second, that it was full of brisket.

I wasn't sure what "brisket" meant, other than it being a bad thing. Catherine demanded I go back to Dr. Powys and request he give us something edible, including some steaks and a few joints that would be easy to roast.

Being conflict-averse, I agreed, of course, and gathering up seventy-five percent of the brisket, headed off to Huw's farm for the showdown. An hour later, I returned with a car full of sirloin and fillet steaks. Peace once again settled on our home.

# 29

# Cock-au-Vin

## November 14, 2004

That weekend I found myself standing in a damp field wearing black steel-capped Wellington boots stained with concrete and a gilet in a colour described by Marks & Spencer as burnt orange but which resembled the off-yellow of a ten-day-old baby's loose stool. I was attempting to talk to Richard Headley's friend, Hector Leopold-Smithers, who was demonstrating perfectly something known as "meercat syndrome" as he desperately pretended to be interested in what I said while his head jerked from side to side and over my shoulder to find someone more influential to talk to.

Anyone vaguely dull, like me, trying to talk to somebody at a conference, party, or other forced social situation, would be familiar with the "meercat" — the colleague who had no interest in talking to you whatever in which a stilted conversation ensued while you were fully aware he or she was scanning the room, keen to get away.

I was in the field because Richard had asked if I'd like to go on a pheasant shoot. Initially, I'd politely declined on the basis I'd never held a shotgun, didn't own a Barbour jacket, and didn't possess tweed trousers. Not to mention that the thought of spending time with Headley's private school chums, Florian, Hector, and Peregrine, filled me with total despair. Thankfully, I told him I had the opportunity to amputate my left arm with an angle grinder, which would be more fun.

When I was nine, my dad owned a rental property, a three-storey Victorian redbrick house with a vast attic that had narrow slit windows, one of which had broken, allowing several pigeons to move in. Dad had an old air pistol he thought would be the perfect weapon to finish off the vermin. However, after ten shots, he'd made no progress but allowed me to have a try. It took most of my strength to cock the pistol and load the pellet. I could barely even lift the gun, weakness being one of my major lifelong characteristics.

I pulled the trigger, whereupon a pigeon that until then had been chatting to his friend about the perfection of their life and what they might be doing that evening, flew down in a spiral, one wing beating, and landed at my feet, blood pumping from its little head. Cocking the gun again, I shot the bird a second time, which had no apparent terminal effect. At that point, I was seized by guilt and panic, and the pigeon's suffering was only ended by the timely intervention of my father, who dispatched the poor creature efficiently.

There was a lot of apologizing and deal-making with God for the rest of the day, and I'd vowed never to harm any creature ever again — barring some insects, of course.

That was the real reason why I'd declined Richard's pheasant shoot. When I'd mentioned this to Catherine, she'd told me not to be so ridiculous, and hence here I was in a damp field with what an uncharitable person would describe as posh twats. I figured I could aim randomly at the sky, hopeful not to be any real danger to the pheasants, which had no doubt been bred solely for this great moment in their lives.

However, I never got to fire the gun, though I did load it. When I turned around to ask what to do next, there was a lot of shouting about why I shouldn't aim a loaded shotgun at a group of people standing in a meadow. So, I decided to sit in Headley's car while they all got rid of their excess testosterone.

This had proven to be a total waste of a Saturday, but it wasn't the day's low point.

That evening, Catherine and I were going out, but I was firmly in the doghouse within ten minutes. Catherine had decided to invite two of her ghastly friends, with ghastly partners, to meet at the Green Dragon for a pub meal. She sensed my reluctance to spend time going out for dinner with Matilda, her old school friend who called herself Tilly, and her husband, Claude, along with a work colleague named Alan Heath, who was bringing Lesley, his new wife.

Claude was a farmer who had been involved in an unfortunate accident during which a pig bit off his genitals when he was seventeen. They had twin girls, both ginger, whom I suspected to be part of the cohort using the special discount ginger sperm the donor clinic was palming off on anyone who fancied cheaper fertilization. Not the good ginger, more a terrible shade that brought to mind a Tamworth pig.

Tilly used to be one hundred and forty pounds but had developed big bones and fluid retention and was now what was known as a woman of size. She had an unfortunate sweating problem that made her permanently look as if she were eating a spicy vindaloo.

My only duty was to act as a polite husband this evening and on no account look down at Claude's crotch or order the coq au vin. That was a little like when you were told "Don't look now" and you immediately *had* to stare. So, my eyes were instantly drawn to Claude's trousers. Catherine fired a glare at me that spoke of two more days in the doghouse. When I ordered the Cumberland sausage, my fate was sealed.

Tilly was a teacher and thus complained incessantly about how hard she worked. She worked with Alan, who taught woodwork and had a strange habit of adding the word *me* to most statements. He agreed that nobody worked as hard as a teacher, and they didn't finish at 3:30 at all. They spent hours per week making lesson plans. Alan said things like "I work ruddy 'ard, me," "I don't finish at three, me," and "I spend ruddy hours making lesson plans, me."

I pointed out that lesson plans couldn't be that time-consuming, since Alan's class was still making the same things now as twenty years ago: a plywood two-dimensional brontosaurus in the first term and a birdhouse in the second and third terms. The dinosaur was cut by Alan on a band saw and given to the students to sand and varnish over the next ten weeks. The birdhouse, similarly, involved minimal input by the students other than glue and varnish.

Alan took umbrage, as did Lesley, who looked to me to be a prop forward in Kilminster's rugby team and was in the first stage of transitioning. There were important questions I needed to ask but which a sharp glance from Catherine told me weren't for this evening. I should clarify, however, that on this suspicion I was entirely incorrect and it was simply that Lesley was a very tall woman with a very deep voice.

Lesley's eyes welled with tears as she supported Alan's protestations about the arduous life of a woodwork teacher, and I realized I'd probably blown all of my points at home. I gained some comfort when Alan went for a pee and Lesley admitted he could be a little defensive about being a woodwork teacher with one arm. I might have omitted to mention that he'd lost his arm while preparing wood for the brontosaurus project and getting his sleeve caught in the band saw. So at least two of the guests tonight were missing a beloved appendage.

Catherine did her best to steer the conversation to safer ground, and I did my best to keep my counsel.

Lesley scratched her beard, blew her nose on a grubby white handkerchief, and gazed at the mucus she'd produced like a medium peering at tea leaves, before giving out a final sob. She rescued the night, however, by changing the subject to talk about Alan's new racing pigeon, Caesar, oddly named after a salad.

The drive home from the Green Dragon was accompanied by the ominous silence the married man knows all too well.

# 30

# VOMIT

## November 15, 2004

The dictionary defines VOMIT as a noun that means "victim of modern imaging technology." My first patient on Monday was Janet Hunter, a middle-aged female who had had a recent amputation. I was being asked for advice about the need for anticoagulation, since she had had a blood clot, a thrombosis, in the past few weeks. She was only in her mid-forties and ran a stable on the edge of town.

Her story was typical of VOMIT. It had all started with a vague feeling of shortness of breath, which with the benefit of hindsight was mild asthma triggered by pollen.

The internet, being a trustworthy source of diagnosis and treatment advice when your hairdresser was unavailable for a more reliable opinion, suggested interstitial lung disease as the ominous diagnosis. It sounded bad, so Janet arranged an urgent appointment with her family doctor.

In the meantime, she took the advice of the online help group run by her hairdresser, which recommended a complementary therapy she could buy online for only £50 — and get two bottles for the price of one … but wait, if she called now, she could get a tube of anti-inflammatory skin cream worth £19.99 as a free gift. Janet began the complementary therapy, derived from the fermented dung of a Himalayan pink salt miner, with some rare Nepalese herbs and tree barks.

Her family doctor couldn't find much wrong with her, and after a thorough examination, recommended an X-ray of her chest. The report came back three days later, advising there was a small area at the right lung base that could be just a rib shadow but would be better reviewed with a chest CT scan. Janet waited four weeks for the CT, which showed no problem with her lungs at all, but a small cyst in the right kidney was visible and would be better imaged with an MRI.

The MRI was booked for three weeks hence, and upon its completion, the recommendation was that a very safe procedure called a percutaneous biopsy would reassure everybody that the renal lesion was as innocent as expected. The biopsy didn't go well. A blood vessel was hit, and Janet found herself having an emergency laparotomy to staunch the bleeding, which happily also confirmed that the renal lesion was entirely benign.

Unfortunately, during her recovery from the laparotomy, Janet suffered a deep-vein thrombosis in her leg. She was started on warfarin to thin the blood. Finally home, Janet restarted her herbal remedy.

However, she slipped on the stairs that evening and twisted her leg, which swelled remarkably. She called her doctor, who assumed this was part of the leg thrombosis and reassured her, unaware she was actually bleeding into her calf secondary to the herbal remedy that had increased the anticoagulant effect of the warfarin.

Janet called her hairdresser, whose admittedly extensive medical knowledge didn't include something nobody had heard of called compartment syndrome, which was caused by bleeding into a tight space like the calf. This was a surgical emergency, because untreated, it could lead to the amputation of a limb.

So, twelve weeks after her pollen-season cough, Janet was now minus half her right leg. Her horse riding was likely to be significantly curtailed — a true case of VOMIT. How she wished she'd never had any medical imaging.

After seeing Janet, my general mood was somewhat dampened. Two cases of acute leukemia later, my mood had sunk even further. Now I sat in the hospital canteen thinking about Richard Headley killing his wife. He'd been interviewed twice but not yet formally charged, though I suspected that was simply a matter of time.

Richard and I were having lunch in the canteen, and I asked him why he'd chosen blunt trauma over the other methods we'd discussed.

"Believe it or not, Brian, I'm not sure I'd ever have had the nerve to kill her. I've imagined her dead for the past year or so, but now that it's actually happened, I think I might miss her."

"Are you trying to tell me it wasn't you?"

"No. Of course, it wasn't. I think it was Milky's mother, Saffron."

Richard went on to explain how he'd gone to look for Therese, knowing she'd been to see the medium. He'd walked in, climbed the stairs, and immediately spotted the body of his wife, clearly dead, with Saffron staring at her skull and holding the crystal ball.

"You told all of this to Inspector McAlister, I assume?"

"Of course. He didn't believe me. Apparently, she's been away visiting her sister in Wales for a few weeks, according to Milky. And I can't deny I was there. I even ran straight into your brother, Harvey, when I left. Then I began to second-guess myself and ask if it was really Therese I'd seen lying there."

During Richard's explanation, I said nothing.

# 31

# The Marble Roll Method

**November 18, 2004**

I stepped out of the shower and reached for a shirt that failed to fit around my slowly increasing abdominal girth. I had to try three before finding one that didn't gape at the naval level.

"I feel like a fat bastard," I said to Catherine.

"I feel the same," she replied.

"No, Kate, you really aren't fat. You still have a perfect figure."

"No, I mean I feel the same — you are a fat bastard."

Catherine always had a way of boosting my self-esteem.

The evening before had been insightful. The marble roll method for assessing excess weight provided a clear, scientific estimate of future cardiac risk. It simply required a marble and a tape measure. The first step was to place the marble four fingerbreadths above the umbilicus, better known as the belly button, then let it roll down the abdomen, and as it launched, an observer marked the spot where the marble hit the floor.

The distance from the end of the big toe to this point, in inches, was the multiplier for risk of a fatal cardiac event in the next decade. Mine came out at five inches, which seemed somewhat worrying, even if the technique was pure fiction.

Thus, I'd commenced another new diet consisting of liquidized spinach and fruit with yoghurt three times a day and was optimistic it would improve my toe-to-marble distance significantly. I gave up milk in coffee, which I assumed would be easy because I'd once heard Catherine say to a friend that when you try black, you never go back.

Harvey, too, seemed a little heavier than he should be and agreed to join me, though he had become somewhat of a doomsayer recently, claiming you didn't need to read a book about future dystopian society because that time was now with us. He whittered on about the least likely scenarios, such as mobile phones being able to track your every move. I told him not to be so ridiculous, since that was never going to happen. His ex-boyfriend, Dennis Greanleaf, had recently left him, and I think Harvey was experiencing some sort of rebound low mood.

Dennis had listened to my suspicions about the number of women in Kilminster with ginger-haired toddlers and my theory that this was all about the price of sperm from donor clinics. Harvey was going to be the manager and Dennis the provider in their own business offering "products" to women in need. I'd seen Harvey with two sets of ice tube trays at the checkout of the local supermarket: he'd mentioned these were a necessary business expense.

Harvey and I had decided to take a regular evening walk twice a week from my home into Kilminster, around the park, and then back again. We'd managed this less often over the past month than planned — only once so far. Today, however, we were committed to get back in the weight-loss game and set off in earnest. Catherine suggested we get some fish and chips on the way back, and I'd worked out that if we increased our speed a little, I'd burn more calories, lose more weight, and thus be able to get myself a battered sausage, as well.

As we entered the Silver Cod, Harvey mentioned the last time he'd been here he had almost been bowled over by Mary Taylor as she rushed out of the door to Norm's upstairs flat.

I frowned. "Oh! I thought it was Richard Headley who ran into you."

"Well, yes, now that you've said it, him, too. But Mary was first and Richard about ten minutes later."

We came out a few minutes later, a white plastic bag in my hand containing three portions of cod and chips, plus a separate wrapped pair of battered sausages we felt we'd eat before getting home while our metabolic rates were higher, and also so Catherine couldn't have anything to say about my lack of self-control.

The following morning clinic was tough having only been allowed ten calories for breakfast. Luckily, it was the birthday of one of the nurses and there was plenty of cake to stave off the hunger pangs crippling me by mid-morning.

Later that day, another drug rep visited me. About three lunchtimes per week one would come, with or without an appointment. Dennis Greanleaf, Harvey's ex, was relatively new to Plus Denario, having started about four months earlier. His predecessor had been fired for failing to achieve the target of seeing each specialist sixteen times per year. I remembered her. She looked a little like a Las Vegas hooker and was so in your face about Nothrombo that I constantly declined her offers to bring me lunch. The thought of spending the time it took to eat a ham sandwich with her was abhorrent.

In earlier days, the length of time for reps to "detail" their doctors was set at eight minutes, which was considered the time it took a doctor to smoke a cigarette. The escape for a smoke was so precious to doctors that seeing reps was a very welcome break in the day. Indeed, there was a Pavlovian response that meeting the rep reminded the doctors of pleasurable activity, and a subconscious link to the drug being peddled could be forged.

I gathered from Dennis, who of course wasn't meant to divulge the contents of the Brian Standish folder he kept in his car, that I was considered Tier 1, meaning I needed extra focus from Plus Denario because I wasn't prescribing as much Nothrombo as I did for its competitor product.

My mind dwelled on what else was in my folder. Pharma reps always seemed to remember that I had children, even the name of my dog and where I vacationed last year. They were like a best friend, except they knew more about me than any of my friends.

Dennis always hung around the patient waiting room, and even if he saw specialists in the distance, that counted as a contact. If they smiled or acknowledged him, that was worth extra points in the day.

Today, he caught me off guard, because rather than ask about blood clots, he questioned me on my knowledge of Powel Syndrome and its treatment with Orgasmia. Dennis had spent the weekend at an intensive course with the training manager, who filled his innocent mind with details of the new disease, though most of the population were now aware of it, thanks to three women's magazines and a campaign by the *Daily Mail* newspaper to increase government spending on Powel Syndrome in the past three months. Indeed, the name then changed over a period of a few days to Chronic Powel Syndrome. A few stalwarts tried to shorten this to CPS until it was pointed out that already meant Crown Prosecution Service.

Professor Powel was the keynote speaker at different conferences, making about £5,000 per week on top of his salary. He also ran a private clinic and had free supplies of the drug in a locked cupboard in his office, which he gave to the patients whose susceptibility to placebo never waned. Interestingly, the probability of a privately referred patient having Chronic Powel Syndrome diagnosed by the professor was one hundred percent. One only needed to have had a gynecological, abdominal, neurological, or musculoskeletal symptoms once in the past year to qualify. And best of all, there were no tests to confirm the diagnosis.

"Do you see many patients with this condition?" Dennis asked me. A classic introductory line by a pharma rep.

I wanted to say I'd never heard of it but didn't wish to appear dumb. "Oh, yes, definitely a few each week."

"Have you had a chance to use Orgasmia yet? Can you help my understanding by telling me which patients you find are best suited to Orgasmia?"

Dennis knew full well I'd never prescribed the drug.

He continued with a charming smile. "I'm hosting an educational event for GPs. I think they'd love to hear about how Powel Syndrome presents in secondary care. We have a set of training slides, and I'd love it if you could be the speaker. We'd pay you a fee, of course. Probably £3,000."

Dennis noticed me hesitate. I really had no interest in this, but £3,000 was enough to go away for a few days. We both knew how this would end. Dress it all up as an educational event and GPs would flock to hear me, mainly because they'd get paid to come and listen. And thus, the mighty pound won the day, and once again I descended from pharma hater to pharma whore. And somewhere along the way I spent an hour or so reading the slides and learning everything about Orgasmia which, of course, was the whole point of the charade.

Dennis left me a few Orgasmia pens, some Post-it notes with the same logo, and the product monograph, all of which we both knew would go into the trash in the next few minutes.

Meanwhile, my investigation into the mystery of the wrong kidney was hampered significantly by the lack of clarity about what had happened before and during the surgery. I was now additionally to review the case of the keyhole surgery that was replaced by a major open cholecystectomy. Christopher Andrews, the anesthetist in the gallbladder case, was, like many of his colleagues, a functioning alcoholic. Perhaps not quite as functional as one would imagine, since he'd begun to moonlight at another hospital, too, owing to his considerable financial difficulties.

The Andrews issue was one of those hindsight-twenty-twenty-vision scenarios in which after the event everybody seemed to know a lot more about him than was apparent at the time. The event in question was that on his way home last week his car left the road and hit a tree. Dr. Andrews found himself in an ambulance admitted to Kilminster Hospital with a broken femur that was pinned the same evening. By the following morning, the mental health team had been called because he was sweating, shaking, and confused. It was assumed he had some sort of infection, so he was given broad-spectrum antibiotics, but to no avail. It required a psychiatrist to see him and to diagnose, within two minutes, that he had delirium tremens from acute alcohol withdrawal.

It wasn't felt that he was a reliable witness for the issue, so the hospital's lawyers suggested we shouldn't mention the name of the anesthetist when we wrote up our report.

# 32

# Haggis and Bagpipes

## November 19, 2004

It was Fraser Cameron's turn to host the Economy Dining Club. Fraser was an obnoxious character who was the senior partner at the family practice where the late Mark Stone had worked. To his credit, Fraser had been voted Family Practitioner of the Year. He was particularly proud of this achievement and chose not to humbly keep quiet about it.

It wouldn't be churlish for me to observe that the award involved a nomination process, and Fraser had chosen to anonymously nominate himself. Not just once. The awards committee, when it met, was amazed to discover three nominations for Fraser and no others across the whole country. Thus, their task was straightforward, and Fraser was honoured for his global medical skills, including diagnostic prowess, patient communication, and research.

We arrived at the Cameron residence where his wife, Elspeth, greeted us and showed us into the front hall to see a life-sized human-shaped cardboard poster on a stand. It featured a photograph of Fraser that he'd brought home from the awards ceremony. Even for a smug bastard, he looked particularly smug and bastardly. Of course, we all smiled and commented on how fun this was.

On offer tonight was haggis, neeps, and tatties, which depending on one's perspective was either a delicious combination of meat, oatmeal, onions, salt, and spices, with turnip and potato, or something akin to cat litter mixed with powdered soup served with tasteless mush, the sort found in a cheap nursing home. I was too polite to let anyone know which side I personally sat.

Fraser and Elspeth had recently completed a major home renovation, and once we'd all arrived, we were given a tour, starting with the master bedroom and en suite bathroom. I noted that the bed had eight pointless cushions on it, all in the Cameron tartan, a West Highland design that, for clarity, looked similar to every other tartan to an uneducated hematologist from Kilminster. There was also a large painting of Mount Eiger on the wall signed by our hostess, Elspeth Cameron.

"This is amazing," I said. "When were you in Switzerland?"

"Never," she replied in her Glaswegian accent, which made my nuts retract into my diaphragm as images of Scotland's fabled rebel William Wallace flashed in my mind. "This is Ben Nevis."

"I went to school with a boy named Ben Nevis," piped up Catherine.

We were then shown into the en suite where there was a mysterious oak trapdoor with a brass Scottish thistle to lift it, revealing a chute to the floor below. Cameron proudly told us how he'd personally designed the chute to allow efficient movement of clothes, such as kilts, sashes, and sporrans, into the laundry room below.

Once we'd moved downstairs, we were, of course, shown the laundry room to reveal the lower end of the chute. To my disappointment, there were no kilts from the floor above, just a pair of jeans, a red sweatshirt, and a pair of white Y-fronts with a shocking fecal stain that will haunt me until my dying day.

Somehow the stain, which resembled a Jackson Pollock painting, interfered with my enjoyment of the meal we consumed in a rather sombre dining room with dark oak panelling and too many pictures of Highland cows. Over the fireplace was a second picture, this time a painting of Fraser Cameron himself. Our dining club meals were meant to be light-hearted and fun every few weeks, but it was going to take a minor miracle to save this one, the more so since Fraser had decided to play Gabriel Fauré's Requiem as we ate.

Fraser then proceeded to tell us about substantial donations he'd made to a range of local charities to remind us of what an all-round great human he was. Quietly, I hoped Mark Stone's fatal condition was contagious.

The host of the Economy Dining Club was entitled to invite one guest outside the normal membership. Fraser and Elspeth had invited Adrianna Whittaker, the well-known *Daily Mail* columnist.

She had an illustrious career based around a single theme. In 1998, she wrote a short piece that was accepted by *Trout and Salmon* magazine. I'd read "The Ten Best Pubs for Salmon Fishermen" shortly after the incident described in my previous book, which I'd penned while recovering from the trauma of the first series of murders in Kilminster. That book had now sold twelve copies.

With the success of "Ten Best Pubs," Adrianna stuck to her theme and wrote for a range of magazines "The Ten Best Walks in the Peak District," "The Ten Best Hotels on a Budget," "The Ten Best Hotels for Your Anniversary," "The Ten Best Hotels for Lovers," "The Ten Vegetables You've Never Tried," and "The Ten Best Wines for Cold Winter Nights." Then she graduated to *Cosmopolitan* where she wrote "The Ten Best Fruits to Make You Horny," and from there her work evolved into racier content.

It was the *Daily Mail*, however, that provided the best income for her, because for it, almost any topic was applicable, provided there were ten to write an article on the subject even if the writer knew mothing about the theme. The British middle class couldn't get enough pieces on coastal walks, wine pairings, coffee grinders, and aluminum saucepans. The *Mail* had discovered that if Adrianna did a feature on something for the home, then the manufacturers might offer sponsorship, too. So, "The Ten Best Wines Under £20 for a Winter Evening" was accompanied by an ad for the same wines and a cut-out voucher for a discount on corkscrews, along with an invitation to join a wine club.

Clearly, if you had a winner, you stuck with it.

As had occurred at the previous dinner party, the women with children started to share stories. Adrianna told us about her sixty-hour labour. Richard Headley, unimpressed, likened giving birth to passing a large, constipated stool, which had the desired effect of simultaneously offending and silencing her. I was quite surprised Richard had agreed to attend this dinner. He was still working and had somehow managed to ignore whispered comments wherever he went.

"Where's Therese tonight?" asked Warwick Tetlow. Was he living on another planet?

"She couldn't get her face to look right," replied Headley to indrawn gasps from most of the guests.

On a roll, Richard mentioned his hemorrhoids and rectal abscess.

"That's not the sort of thing to discuss at a dinner party," Elspeth objected indignantly.

"Well, it's no worse than learning that Adrianna's vulva looks like Gandolph's face," Headley fired back. "Though since sitting in your hot tub last week I think my abscess burst. It's been a great deal better for the past few days. Whereas Adrianna's clunge will never look any better."

Even I thought this might have gone a little too far.

The spark of the night that had barely glowed from the outset was now well and truly extinguished. But on came dessert, which was profiteroles with chocolate sauce. The Y-fronts returned to the front of my mind, and I decided to pass.

The evening ended with Fraser describing his sporting prowess, his triumphs at golf, his recent wins at tennis, and how he'd recently bought a horse and turned out to be a natural equestrian. He then slipped out and returned wearing a kilt and with his bagpipes, which reminded me that Catherine and I had to get home urgently for the babysitter.

# 33

# The Beef Sin Comes to Light

## November 22, 2004

On Monday, I was in the hospital canteen in the far corner hoping not to be noticed and to have thirty minutes without another human being near me. So, of course, I was immediately joined by an idiot. Stuart Brennan had no sooner sat down opposite me than he loudly blew his nose, with the sound of the last dregs seemingly being pumped from a septic tank. He then picked his ear intently, wiping whatever ended up on his finger on the inside of his jacket.

"I've just done a poo in the exact shape of a question mark," he proudly announced.

I warmly congratulated him.

Next, he added, "Then there's the eternal poo."

I should have known better, but I had to ask, "What's an eternal poo?"

"One where you use a whole roll of toilet paper and still can't get your bum clean. I can't work out the scientific problem causing it." Then he shifted topics. "What part of a woman shouldn't move when dancing?"

Before I could hear the answer to this important question, we were interrupted by Mrs. Macaron, our CEO, who asked if I could spare a moment later in the day so she could get an update on my

Desmond Leech investigation. Her arrival presented the perfect opportunity to leave Stuart, so I eagerly leaped up, grabbing my tray to slide into a big silver trolley.

"Right now would be perfect," I told her. "Sorry, Stuart."

"Her bowels!" he shouted as I left the dining room with Mrs. Macaron, who had completed her sponsored macron bake and disappointed me by reminding me that I owed her some money.

Having paid up, I agreed it was reasonable to suggest to Desmond that he take a paid leave of absence while the two main cases were dealt with. I promised to find the right moment to speak to him.

When I returned to the surgical ward, I found my patient who had been away from her bed the previous few times I'd tried to locate her. As always, there was the smell of urine as I walked into the ward. My patient was in the middle bed on the left in a six-bed bay.

The curtains were drawn around the adjacent bed. They failed to close properly, giving a clear view of an elderly lady with thin, straggly white hair who weighed about ten pounds and wore a light pink vest and little else. She was sitting on a commode, which explained the overwhelming fecal smell that threatened to attach itself to my clothes like cheap aftershave.

The nurses and health-care assistants were to be congratulated for their pretense that they couldn't hear the dismal wails for help. They were also oblivious to a mind-numbing, incessant beep from an intravenous infusion alarm declaring it to be complete. Help was unlikely to come. Her assigned nurse had forgotten her and was probably now on a break, no doubt planning a hen party to Ibiza where she and eight others were to dress as sheep. The bride, of course, would be Little Bo Peep.

At the desk was Kathy De'ath, a nephrologist who had accepted the appointment after her predecessor's murder. She was a woman of infinite patience and kindness but was visibly disgruntled today because the medical manager and his sidekick, along with a new manager with responsibility for wait-time targets, had cornered her to demand she run an evening wait-list initiative clinic, which was the hospital's way of flying below the quality radar.

"We're all in this together," insisted the manager, who would certainly be home by 4:30 p.m.

"I'm sorry. It's simply not possible. I have a child to pick up."

"Your childcare arrangements don't seem a reasonable explanation for your patients having to wait sixteen weeks to be seen."

"No, the explanation would be that nine hundred new referrals per year and two thousand review patients, along with one in eight on call, might be enough for two to reasonably achieve. So why not appoint a second nephrologist?"

One nil to Kathy.

"The alternative is perhaps that we add a community hospital clinic in Aston Leonard. There's a weekly Friday afternoon slot available for you to run your clinic," replied the manager. "It's only a forty-five-minute drive."

One all.

Aston Leonard was thirty miles away, and the Friday was empty because an overrunning clinic that day wasn't top of the wish list for most staff.

To her credit, Kathy didn't break. "Let me see if I can get childcare" was her reply, at which point she returned the patient's notes and left the ward, leaving the manager unsure if the goal had been achieved.

Later that day, I was almost in the doghouse once more. Catherine and I had been sitting all evening watching one of those shows in which humans with minimal talent try to become famous. And in which if they were precocious children or had some form of special needs, they were guaranteed to get to the next round.

Catherine kept doing this peculiar twitch of her head to the left, gazing at the French windows, and I'd taken the hint by drawing the curtains. The head twitch continued, though, and began to seem a little more impatient, then Catherine suddenly almost yelled at me, "You haven't even noticed we have new curtains!"

To be absolutely honest, she was technically correct. To be more honest, she was totally correct. But whoever looked at curtains? Yet I was able to successfully pull off the double bluff by saying, "Hah! I knew you wanted me to comment and was determined to pretend I hadn't noticed."

In her innocence, Catherine found this extremely amusing and confessed she knew I'd detected them earlier in the evening. So, with great hilarity, we continued to watch the awful talent show and I inwardly celebrated dodging a bullet for a change. These were the golden moments in which there was little to be gained by complete honesty.

About twenty minutes later, Rianne Kyle called asking to speak to Catherine. When my wife got on the phone, Rianne asked her excitedly what event we must be planning, since she'd seen me in the supermarket a couple of weeks ago buying enough steaks for about a hundred people. And just like that, all my gains for the day were wiped out.

# 34

# The Breast Milk of Human Kindness

## November 27, 2004

A few days later, on Saturday, all was forgiven and Catherine seemed to be in a buoyant mood.

"I think I'll tidy up the garage today," I said as I prepared breakfast.

"Oh, very funny," she replied. "I know you haven't forgotten that we're heading down to Exeter."

"Exeter?" I asked.

"Yes," she continued with a hint of menace in her eyes. "To meet Ian and Grace."

Ian Beaney, as I'd said, was her brother, the veterinary surgeon in Truro. He was easy to talk to and one of the more genial members of Catherine's family, though there were many times I got the sense of shady dealings concerning him. Grace, his wife, was a little less straightforward and didn't seem to match Ian at all. I'd say she didn't like him at all. She voted Green Party, ate tofu, and wore tie-dyed clothes. Their family was a little younger than ours, with children of five and seven. The five-year-old was still being breast-fed. It often spontaneously stopped playing with its Lego and rushed over to Grace to suckle on a teat for a quick slurp, then returned to the Lego.

Catherine told me I shouldn't be concerned about things that were none of my business, though I had to confess there was something here that seemed a little off, and tolerating Grace trying to take us captive to her viewpoint on all things "green" made me want to leave the car engine running for half an hour just to ruin the ozone layer.

So, the day would be a write-off unless I could position myself next to Ian and out of Grace's line of sight. What lay in store was a three-hour drive to meet them for a pub lunch and a walk with children who couldn't manage more than two hundred yards before they complained.

When we arrived, I was disappointed to learn, through the power of smell, that Grace had a new natural deodorant. The scent of body odour was testament to the fact that wiping a lump of granite in one's armpit was unlikely to be a triumph.

We met in a café in the centre of the city. To my delight, Ian was in fine form. He'd just come back from a conference in the United States where apparently the hotel, and every eating establishment he frequented, offered him a twenty percent discount just because of his job.

"As soon as I told them I was a vet, they thanked me for my service and reduced the bill," he said, laughing. "No idea why."

I noticed that Ian drove a new Range Rover and appeared to be financially flush, with frequent work-related and apparently lucrative travel to Europe. However, his vet licence was still suspended, though I didn't mention that.

Halfway through the lunch, a tall, good-looking Black man in his early twenties came over to our table and was about to speak when Ian leaped up and dragged him to the foyer where there were some rapid words followed by both of them leaving for a couple of minutes.

"I look after his cat," puffed a breathless Ian as he returned to our table.

"Quite the coincidence he arrived at the same café as you, two hundred miles from home, and appeared to know where to find you," I observed.

"Small world," said Catherine, who could sometimes be less inquisitive than a situation demanded.

Nothing more was said for the next ten minutes, though by his urgent expression, Ian was clearly telling me to leave the company of the women and engineer a meeting in the washroom.

Within thirty minutes, I was £500 worse off, and on top of that, Catherine offered to pay for all the food.

"It must have been a tough few months when Ian couldn't work," she declared, apparently oblivious to the Range Rover and her brother's flashy watch. "We'll get this."

But perhaps at this point I should go back in time a little in Ian's story.

# 35

# My Brother-in-Law's Story

Darren Greanleaf had been offered a job by Ian collecting horse semen from France after losing his job in the jeweller's shop. Greanleaf was Dennis's brother, who was Harvey's ex. We met him at the beginning of my tale. Ian was heavily involved in the horse semen venture, a sure sign there was a shady component. With his veterinary connections and lack of a licence to practice, he'd embraced the world of horse racing, particularly the organized crime side of it.

Due to history and family connections, I was required to maintain Ian Beaney in a state of affection. I'd met Catherine through my brother-in-law, who was a year my senior at school. Unlike me, he seemed to excel effortlessly in whatever he applied himself to. "Effortless" described him well, since he rarely concerned himself with anything unless it was unethical, illegal, or just stupid.

I hovered in the band of mediocrity throughout school, seldom achieving anything. I did win three chess matches when I was fifteen, much to my own and everybody else's surprise. Sadly, chess didn't raise one's chances of acquiring a girlfriend, it seemed.

Meanwhile, Ian could catch a cricket ball, score a try in rugby, and maintain himself comfortably in the top tenth percentile when it mattered. More irritatingly, he possessed the talent of charming his way into the affections of all teachers, such that he was duly elected head boy in the sixth form. Among the many honours of being head boy came a little sew-on patch for the breast of one's blazer. It was only a modest version of the school coat of arms, but it spoke of high achievement in one's life to date and the potential for greatness in adulthood. A glance at Ian's blazer told any boy in the school that this was the head boy and senior prefect, who wielded enough power to mete out punishments for infractions, though to my recollection Ian never took advantage of this perk.

Everything came crashing down to earth about four weeks before the end of summer term. One of the privileges of being a sixth former was to be allowed to walk into town over lunch, a fairly pointless honour since it took twenty minutes and meant heading back almost as soon as one arrived. Halfway to town was a small bridge over the river, and somehow Ian's friend, Doughnut Dunnet — so-called because he looked as if he'd partaken of too many of said snack — persuaded him it would be tremendous fun to jump into the river from the bridge. It was only a fifteen-foot drop. The water would be warm, and it would be easy to climb out. Ian agreed this would be totally sensible and immediately climbed onto the bridge parapet and launched himself into the water without taking off an item of clothing. Doughnut followed, discovered that trying to swim fully clothed was challenging, and was rescued thirty yards downstream by a couple in a rented rowing boat. Dunnet elected to take the afternoon off.

Ian decided to return to school rather than dry off and reflect on his idiocy. When he arrived at his double maths class soaked through, the teacher, Mr. Travis, said not a word. This was followed by French and again no words were spoken. It was felt by most of us that Ian had gotten away with the episode until school assembly the following morning, a rather formal occasion in which a thousand boys sat bored stiff while the teachers took a seat onstage behind our headmaster, Horace Smythe, who spoke like Noël Coward and acted like a Nazi doctor about to experiment on his next victim.

Various announcements were made, followed by some pretentious Latin that always indicated the end of assembly: *Florescunt pueri scholae Sancti Decani*; "Flourish boys of St. Dean's School." The boys enjoyed pronouncing the first word with inappropriate emphasis.

Then, instead of being dismissed, we heard Smythe invite Ian to climb the stairs to the stage. I might have omitted to say that all students were referred to solely by their last names.

Ian rose from his chair to the sound of nine hundred and ninety-nine boys whispering that it was something to do with jumping off the bridge the day before. After Smythe asked Ian to stand by him, the headmaster ceremoniously produced a genuine surgical scalpel from the podium in front of him and proceeded to cut off the little coat of arms from Ian's blazer. My future brother-in-law was then invited to return to his seat.

To Ian's credit, once he was out of the line of sight of the headmaster, he flashed a huge smile to the rest of the school. I recalled no words being spoken throughout this court-martial, though I did see the chemistry teacher grin at his colleague about the ridiculous spectacle. Finally, a rather unpleasant boy named Ashley O'Grady, who had the worst acne in the school, was asked to ascend to the stage where the little bit of cloth was formally handed to him for his mother to sew on that night.

"Your new head boy," announced Smythe, and he started to clap. The Latin teacher behind him, who I estimated to be seventy-eight years old, jerked awake and began to clap but then realized none of his teaching colleagues and none of the boys were joining in, so he quickly stopped and tried to make it look as if he'd just been adjusting his tie.

By then, Ian had already secured a place at veterinary school, so no longer being head boy was of little significance to him, other than his parents' shame should they ever find out. From what I subsequently gathered, they were never aware of it. On my part, I tucked away what happened at school with Ian just in case I ever needed to discredit him in front of his parents — one never knew with families.

Ian was hardly a model student at veterinary school, either, but there was a rumour that he met the dean of the veterinary school exiting a house of ill repute in Cirencester just as my brother-in-law was walking in. From that moment on, his degree was in no doubt.

Had he not euthanized the beloved spaniel, Rusty, who had attended for his nails to be cut, Ian would still have his licence.

Sadly, his suspension, initially temporary, seemed likely to be permanent after it emerged that a further complaint had arisen from an elderly widow who claimed Ian had offered to waive her invoice for treating her cat if she agreed to leave him her grandfather clock and sideboard in her will. If only the college knew the *real* depths of his behaviour.

Ian had received a record number of complaints against him that were being dealt with by his regulatory body. The majority of the complaints, while possibly completely reasonable, were dismissed owing to a lack of robust evidence. The most egregious of these was that he'd been accused of consulting with humans and giving them drugs only licensed for animals. In particular, there was a range of anti-inflammatory drugs that were either not available to humans or were substantially cheaper for animals, which he was happy to source and pass on for a reasonable fee to a number of regular clients in the town.

Another accusation was that he was signing off on false pedigree certificates for dogs, cats, and horses for appropriate fees. The challenge here was that most of the people requesting this service were already utterly dishonest themselves, and the college found it difficult to collect enough reliable evidence to take the case forward.

Then there were the usual complaints, which I imagine most vets expect, that he was overcharging or over-recommending a range of investigations and treatments. Ian's perspective was that he was running an expensive business with high rents, a veterinary nurse, and a receptionist, who also served as his lover.

Ian confided more of his activities with me than I cared to know. Thursday afternoon was a half-day closing. As soon as the front door was locked, he joined his receptionist in one of the examination rooms. Thursday afternoon sex — referred to as TAS in the office calendar — had been going on for about eighteen months. Because the stainless-steel examination tables were both cold and uncomfortable, Sally had brought with her a deck chair and a washable cushion. Ian was besotted, while Sally was more transactional in her planning but could do a very good impression of also being besotted. She was also an expert in persuading the owners of beloved pets to have X-rays, blood work, and vaccines that weren't strictly needed, so she was a valuable asset even without TAS.

Sally was the proud owner of a Bengal cat named Pandora, though it was actually a male. This cat was the only male in a litter Ian had delivered by Caesarean section eighteen months earlier. Somehow, he'd accidentally only given the owner four of the kittens. The male he kept and gave to his receptionist, who was running a successful business on the side charging £800 a go for stud services, a system she'd watched Ian develop in his role of chief veterinarian to the Mannbury Stud.

Lord Rivermeade, well-known owner of the world-famous Mannbury Stud, was said to have raised the finest racehorses in England and Continental Europe. It was rumoured that Her Majesty Queen Elizabeth II had asked him if his racehorse Sir Godfrey might sire a foal for her. After producing three Ascot winners, Sir Godfrey's seed was in demand and was valued at £26 million per gallon, though of course it was sold in smaller amounts known as straws. Every ejaculation was worth more than £1 million.

And who was the vet contracted to run the whole enterprise? Ian Beaney, who was quick to realize that by claiming an ejaculated volume twenty-five millilitres less than what had been produced, he could make close to £250,000 every time Sir Godfrey achieved equine orgasm.

Soon, Ian was heavily involved in the illegal trafficking of horse semen, and that was how the contacts were found for the import of the same product, though Ian was well aware both French and British regulatory bodies had him in their sights. Thus, Ian found a courier and created layer upon layer of plausible deniability.

He wasn't overly concerned, since he held £7 million in overseas accounts that he and Sally would eventually spend when Ian finally plucked up the courage to desert his wife. I wondered if he might ever regret that Sally had the full details of his offshore accounts and also that she and Ian's wife shared more information about their lives than he knew.

It was only recently, after his suspension, that the export side of things dried up because he was no longer able to work for Lord Rivermeade. So, Ian employed Darren Greanleaf as a courier to collect straws of semen for the U.K. market and forward them onward to the United States.

After the first successful collection of racehorse semen went without a hitch, the business model was believed to be solid. There followed a lucrative arrangement with five successful journeys in the bag. For each one, Darren made £500. But the sixth journey met with complications.

Darren collected the tube containing two hundred millilitres of the equine potion, and as on the previous five missions, put it into his insulated coffee mug. He took lunch in a pleasant café on the edge of Nice: croque monsieur and a strong café au lait. By now, he'd timed his return to the airport perfectly.

On this occasion, however, as he was passing confidently through the gate holding his coffee and with no hand luggage, he was stopped and told he couldn't take more than one hundred millilitres of liquids through. "You can't take this through," said the border guard. "It's too much liquid." His face looked as if he would have liked to add, "You dumb *rosbif*!"

Flustered, Darren apologized, performed a one-hundred-and-eighty-degree turn, and hurried back toward the departure hall. He was certain the border guard had clocked him coming through in the same way in five previous weeks; his luck was likely turning.

Darren could have decanted the semen into a smaller container, but he didn't have one. He could have put the smaller jar in his pocket and passed through again, but he didn't consider that, either.

Instead, he poured €25,000 worth of racehorse semen down the toilet and headed back to the gate where he caught the return plane to Gatwick, a rapidly evolving new plan in mind.

Two hours later, he pulled into the Esso filling station where he could see his contact, Ian the suspended vet, parked by the air pump pretending to check his tire pressures. Darren quickly parked next to Ian's Range Rover, a new purchase that month, and produced his insulated mug. At that moment, three police patrol cars screeched onto the station forecourt, and six officers ran toward Ian and Darren.

There was much yelling, much feigned confusion, and two sets of handcuffs. The officer in charge smugly opened the insulated mug and drew out the translucent tube filled with an opaque white liquid. “Stallion spunk,” the officer said with a smirk. “You’re nicked.”

At the police station, Darren’s offer to drink the offending liquid, which he insisted was yoghurt, was met with disgust and a thump in the right kidney. But three weeks later when the analysis was complete, all charges were dropped, since there was no law against carrying a small probiotic yoghurt in an insulated mug.

Darren was pleased that he hadn’t carried out his alternate plan, reflecting that two hundred millilitres of stud semen would be challenging to replace, and of course human semen would be less likely to fertilize a mare in heat.

Ian was £2,000 down on the deal but seemed remarkably philosophical about the loss of a sweet profit, considering that his suspension was now over and he’d escaped a potential custodial sentence thanks to the quick thinking of Darren, who was somewhat economical with the truth about how and why the original package had been replaced by the yoghurt.

That was why a handsome Black semen smuggler from London was visiting a Truro vet in a café in Exeter to collect £500 for one yoghurt.

And I, Brian Standish, was somehow on the hook for this because my brother-in-law urgently beckoned me to the toilet to ask if I could lend him £500. He’d already predicted my next words by pointing out an ATM almost directly across the road.

# 36

# FANCY A YOGHURT?

## NOVEMBER 29, 2004

I'd just gotten off a call with Plus Denario, which had invited me to a medical investigators' meeting. At first, I was thrilled, figuring I was very much at the cutting edge. Sadly, by the end of the call, I was filled with doubts to the point that I might never use Orgasmia or any of their other drugs ever again.

Essentially, the plan sounded noble. Some post-launch data would be collected by setting up an Orgasmia Registry in which patients I prescribed the drug to would enter the "study" and report back on their progress for a few months. They'd get regular encouraging calls from the organizing team and would be paid for their involvement. So, dropping out of the study would cost them, of course. For every patient I enrolled, I'd get a large investigator's fee; and for every monthly form I sent in, I'd get more. All of that would increase my income by at least twenty percent.

But not long after the call, I remembered I was a hematologist, not a Powel Syndrome specialist, and that for every £1,000 I made, Plus Denario would pocket £10,000. I'd read in the newspapers that the company was already past £500 million in sales, which meant that even in the worst-case scenario, in which the regulator fined it for breaching regulations on pharmaceutical products, the fine would be dwarfed by the profits. Plus Denario seemed to be following the same marketing strategy that Purdue had pursued for oxycontin. What could possibly go wrong?

So, I performed a one-hundred-and-eighty-degree turn and walked away from the opportunity. I even threw my sponsored pen into the trash. No sooner had I replaced the phone in its cradle than it rang again.

I was getting what I felt to be an unfair amount of anger from a patient who had had difficulty phoning through to my secretary. Sadly, she had, in fact, gotten through by phone and my secretary had failed me by forwarding the call to me. It seemed the caller had actually forgotten the clinical reason for contacting me because she spent at least five minutes explaining to me why the hospital hematology department, my secretary, and I were utterly useless.

Foolishly, I suggested she try using email instead of the phone. The caller told me she "didn't believe in email," whatever that meant. She denied having any trappings of twenty-first-century life such as a cellphone or a computer, though I suspected she was exaggerating her antediluvian qualifications.

"Do you have a car, or do you prefer riding a horse instead?" I asked her.

"Now you're just being facetious, Dr. Standish."

"Well, put your complaint in writing, attach it to a carrier pigeon, and send it to me."

It was with a feeling of great relief that she ended the call, ranting that she was going to make an official complaint. I never did discover why she'd called in the first place. Perhaps her fate would be the same as that in the old music hall song about an old woman who swallowed a fly, and she, too, would die. That would offer a little peace at least. Checking my notes on her later that day, I realized the glacier-like complaints process wouldn't be complete before God had called her.

And now I felt guilty for thinking like that. My secretary came through and asked if I had burnout. That was her subtle way of telling me I'd crossed a line.

"No, I just can't bear even listening to her whining voice. It makes me want to tie an anvil to her legs and throw her off a boat."

She raised an eyebrow and departed. Perhaps I was getting a little stressed, after all.

Ironically, I was invited to become a member of the hospital complaints committee the same week. Despite the woeful state of health care, meaningful complaints were surprisingly few. Most were completely fatuous, perhaps thirty or so per week. Many were about wait times, of course, which were largely outside our control. Some were about elderly parents receiving suboptimal care, and these were more concerning, though often, like wait times, the issue came down to resources and a workforce losing the joy of the profession.

Some were about specific doctors or their secretaries who had failed to return calls in the ninety-minute time frame most patients seemed to expect, as if the staff were lying around the place like dozing cats waiting for something to do. I wondered if my own stroppy patient had sent anything in yet.

Occasionally, medical procedures met with complications. That was a statistical certainty, not negligence or medical error, but try explaining the laws of probability to the average complainant.

Most complaints came directly from patients, a few from lawyers. These were easier in some respects, since they had to follow specific protocols, whereas the others could possibly be addressed with a carefully crafted letter indicating sympathy without liability.

The wrong kidney complaint had already escalated through the hospital's lawyers. Today, we also had to discuss how to investigate a stillbirth, review a minor post-operative wound infection, respond to three complaints about the lack of parking spaces, one about the presence of peanuts in the League of Friends shop, and another about Dr. Headley refusing to stop wearing aftershave to which a patient claimed a deathly allergy. I'd seen the same patient walking through the local department store without collapsing pulseless to the floor. This lack of corpses around the perfume counters of Kilminster's shops made me skeptical.

After discussing and mainly agreeing on how to deal with most complaints, we had to sit with the recent widower of a patient who had died three weeks earlier, having been diagnosed with pancreatic cancer only ten days before her death. Her bereaved husband, a rather frail, wealthy local business owner in his early seventies, was accompanied by his daughter, probably in her late twenties, who wore a short skirt, perhaps three inches below her crotch, and a peculiar top without arms I later learned was called a "boob tube."

They started to clutch hands and kiss each other during the meeting, at which point it was clear that in the three weeks it had taken for his wife's body to cool down, he'd fallen in love a second time and this wasn't his daughter but his new fiancée. Such was the power of Cupid. Romance was a truly beautiful thing, and the man's millions of pounds in the bank, of course, were of no relevance to her falling so rapidly in love with him.

The puzzling aspect of the complaint was that it had nothing to do with the dead woman's care. The couple explained that they felt there should be a way to avoid walking out through the main hospital entrance after receiving bad news and why couldn't a dedicated exit be built along with a free parking area for the recently bereaved. We agreed to look into this urgently, and the two of them seemed placated.

After the meeting, as I headed to my car, my cellphone rang in my pocket. Ian Beaney had a new proposal.

To his credit, my brother-in-law was an efficient businessman. Following the near-disaster when Darren had somehow disposed of the racehorse semen — Ian never knew the full story, of course — Catherine's brother had changed the import model, inspired by Darren's genius. What happened then was that a well-known French yoghurt manufacturer, Happy Cow, better known as La Vache Heureuse, would unknowingly import the illegal racehorse product disguised as a strawberry crème fraîche and occasionally an overripe brie. Darren's role was to smuggle the product into the country, which proved straightforward — €50 to the driver of the refrigerated truck each time, and a further €50 to be given access to the truck to collect the top eight yoghurts before they were sent to the supermarkets.

Out of twenty imports so far, the semen had been retrieved in eighteen shipments. Two had gone astray, one to a Sainsbury's store in Basingstoke and one to a hotel in York. No complaints were ever forthcoming. Ian told me there had been one other yoghurt that went missing, and I recalled a few weeks earlier my brother-in-law asking us to take care of a tray of yoghurts, unaware at the time he thought he was being followed by the police and wanted to get rid of the evidence until the heat was off. Those who have eaten enough French soft cheese will understand how the dairy-disguise method might have gone unnoticed. With a shudder, I once again remembered the yoghurts we'd disposed of and Ian's reaction a few weeks earlier.

Ian had been reading about Powel Syndrome and had quickly realized that many of his clients' pets, be they cats, dogs, or budgerigars, were suffering from canine, feline and avian Powel Syndrome. "All we need is the drug," he explained. "If you could handle that end of things, we'll make a fortune."

I suggested that since my brother's ex, Dennis, was Darren's brother and worked for Plus Denario, maybe he could bypass me. Knowing the pharmaceutical industry, I very much doubted this possibility had escaped the notice of Ian and Darren, and I suspected even now they were trying to work out what price point most pet owners would find bearable for their beloved animals.

"Mind you," I added, "it's only a sugar molecule with a couple of side chains added. You could just invent your own complementary therapy for pets and keep all the profits."

That clearly inspired Ian. "Brian, you're a genius," he gushed before hanging up.

# 37

# POTENTIAL INHERITANCE

## DECEMBER 3, 2004

It was Friday. I arrived home, expecting an evening of peace and hoping not to interact with any human other than Catherine. So, it was understandable that I was somewhat crestfallen to see that Emily Harrison had dropped in. She was a garrulous creature who lived on the other side of Kilminster and had been accompanying Catherine to a pottery class ever since they'd met at one of our Economy Dining Club parties.

Emily could speak for two hours without drawing breath. She'd dyed her hair slightly pink, which to me implied a borderline personality disorder. Regretfully, she'd always been incapable of reading the signs that it was time to leave. Even if I walked to the front door and opened it, she'd follow, waffling on about the two-for-one sale at a Kilminster clothing store, yet not quite step over the threshold and allow the door to be firmly closed behind her.

She mysteriously laughed at most of what I said in a disturbingly high-pitched giggle, a little like Woody Woodpecker's but more grating. She lived alone, which didn't surprise me. Originally, I felt I'd perfected comedy and would be quite buoyed by her cheerful response. With time, however, I learned she'd probably laugh if I told her the cat had just died.

This trait had recently developed a whole new troublesome element after we bought a new sofa. Emily had never been reluctant to tell anybody, even, I suspected, a total stranger on the bus, that whenever she laughed a bit of pee came out. I recalled her oversharing her stress incontinence issue when the late Mark Stone hosted our first Economy Dining Club get-together. Since she usually sat on the sofa near my end when she visited, I had to adopt a look of grave misery whenever I saw her lest she pollute the cushions. That evening, I'd made a mental note to sit elsewhere and figured I should eventually invest in buying some Scotchgard or perhaps a thick tarpaulin the next time she came by.

Then my phone rang. It was the manager of the residential care home where Auntie Jean lived. He spoke with a rather irritating, whispery voice in an unsuccessful attempt to sound serious and concerned. The effect was somewhat negated by the fact that he was clearly watching television. While talking to me, he paused just as a football goal was scored. Suffice to say, he was hoping I'd drive up that evening, owing to a significant decline in Auntie Jean's health over a matter of four or five hours. He'd called the doctor who covered the home and would update me by cellphone on my journey up.

My immediate reaction should have been intense concern for Auntie Jean. I was ashamed to admit, however, that my first thought was that I was likely to be the beneficiary of her estate should she die. Within ninety seconds, I'd already calculated that we might inherit enough to pay off all our debts, then take a cruise and buy a new garden shed with what remained. Quickly, I tucked these uncharitable thoughts into the back of my mind and adopted a sombre face as I turned to inform Catherine I was going to head up straight away. She was listening to Emily tell her about a friend's cat with a skin disease.

"Sorry to interrupt, Catherine. That was Auntie Jean's care home. They've asked me to drive up tonight. Apparently, she's really ill."

Emily hooted with laughter and probably dampened my couch a little more in the process.

"It could be really serious," I added, hoping Emily would calm down.

She laughed again, Catherine jumped up to help me pack a bag, and Emily followed us to relate the story of her ex-husband Tim's root canal.

"Well, if she falls off her perch," said Catherine, "we might be able to pay off some of our debts. And if there's anything left, I'd like to buy a kiln for my pottery."

"That's a terrible thing to say!" I said, looking suitably horrified at her. "I can't believe your mercenary mind immediately goes to inheriting her money."

# 38

# Deep Heat

## December 3, 2004

It took me three and a half hours to get to the residential care home. The roads were clear and the weather dry. The manager had gone home but had told me he'd left a message with the evening staff at reception to meet me. Of course, there was nobody there when I arrived. I waited, coughing loudly for about five minutes, then noticed a door saying STAFF ONLY. Gently knocking, I opened the door, then quickly wished I'd waited to be invited in. A man sitting on the desk faced me with his trousers down, legs apart, spraying Deep Heat muscle rub onto his testicles while reading a gentlemen's magazine. He almost fell off the desk when he saw me and muttered something incoherent about a sports injury.

Once he'd composed himself, he was able to tell me that Auntie Jean had been admitted to Scarborough General Hospital with suspected septicemia. I called Catherine, who suggested I make up a bag of essentials from her drawers to take into the hospital.

"What should I pack?" I asked.

"Are you really that useless?" replied Catherine rhetorically.

"Okay," I said. "I'll pack a pair of knickers and a toothbrush."

"What … and nothing else?"

"Well, what should I pack?" I repeated.

"Underwear, bra, a comfortable blouse and cardigan. And maybe some slacks."

"What the heck are slacks?"

"And maybe take her a book to read, too," added Catherine.

I found a small overnight case. There was something remarkably intrusive about rifling through a relative's drawers in search of clothes. This was a woman who had led a remarkable life. She'd never married or had children but had had a successful career in marketing that had left her comfortably wealthy. Over the years, Auntie Jean had recounted many stories of exotic travel during her lifetime. It thus seemed odd that everything she owned could now be found in four hundred square feet of a care home room. I found a pair of beige knickers made of some sort of shiny material. Carefully avoiding the gusset, I used a ballpoint pen to lift them out of the drawer and into the case. Next, I quickly located everything else she'd need and threw in the book from her bedside table.

The hospital was only about fifteen minutes away. However, it took a further hour before anyone was able to tell me where to find Auntie Jean. I was finally told she was in the medical admissions unit. Supposedly, visitors weren't allowed there and the best thing I could do was to phone in the morning, by which stage she'd be on one of the wards. I left the case with an auxiliary nurse and walked out of the hospital doors, suddenly feeling overwhelmingly tired and realizing I hadn't planned anywhere to sleep that night. Neither had I brought any spare clothes or a toothbrush for myself.

It didn't take long for me to grasp that I hadn't brought my wallet, either. I was slightly anxious about calling Catherine to admit to my failings and thus made my way back to the care home to sleep in Auntie Jean's room. I used her toothpaste on my finger to clean my teeth, making a mental note to myself to take the toothpaste into the hospital, since I'd forgotten to pack it. I needed to fill the car up, too, and would have to borrow some money from Auntie Jean, since I'd left in such a hurry and didn't have a credit or debit card with me or enough cash. I looked around her room for her purse but couldn't spot it.

There was a small desk in the room, and I opened the top drawer. In it was a rectangular tin can about nine by six inches. Inside were newspaper clippings from many years ago about the corpse of a baby found under the floorboards in the attic of a vicarage close to Norwich during a renovation. It had been speculated that a maid in the house had given birth to the baby in the late 1800s and that it had died right away. It seemed odd that my aunt had saved these. In addition, there were some black-and-white photos of two young girls holding a toddler.

Each room in the care home had a small kitchenette. I spied Auntie Jean's purse on the side there, and feeling slightly guilty and intrusive, I borrowed some money from it.

The following morning, I made my way back to the hospital and found Auntie Jean's ward easily. She was sitting in a chair by the bed, toast crumbs and marmalade around her mouth, appearing completely well. *So, no fortune to inherit — yet*, I thought, but had to admit I was rather fond of Auntie Jean.

"Take me home, Brian," she demanded.

I hesitated briefly, realizing I had no appetite to lose an argument with a woman more than a match for me, and agreed that if the medical team was happy, I'd do so.

She was already rising from the chair. "Damn, the medical team. I've already signed my own discharge against medical advice. And I need to get home because my back's killing me and I've got a can of Deep Heat in my room, which is the only thing that helps."

# 39

# Emotional Reunion

## December 7, 2004

Richard Headley had a new cardiology colleague, Barnaby Whittington-Mills. He brought him with him to the Green Dragon, which somewhat bothered me, unreasonably, as I'd begun to enjoy our weekly cribbage game over a pint of Ghost Ship. I felt vaguely threatened. Mind you, to be seen with Headley nowadays was to be observed cavorting with a murderer, if the Kilminster gossip were to be believed.

From what I gathered, Richard and Barnaby had gone to the same elite school, Winchester, albeit twenty years apart. They both wore the same high-end Johnnie Boden clothes and engaged in that irritating banter the pheasant-shooting brigade adopted. Worse still, they described themselves as Old Wykehamists, though I had no idea how Winchester turned into Wykeham. Actually, I figured it was a type of wizard and suggested that perhaps they both got their wands from Diagon Alley. The pair stared at me blankly, clearly unimpressed that once again exclusive privilege was totally lost on me and also telling me that, in future, references to Harry Potter would fail.

Barnaby was equally unimpressed when, having informed me about Winchester School's traditions, I made a tasteless joke about kissing the Founders' Ring, a centuries' old tradition at the school that was a source of amusement to those who hadn't attended. "Philistine," he muttered, cramming pork scratchings into his mouth at the same time, half of them falling onto his pink cashmere V-neck pullover.

I was about to say something full of wisdom and gravitas when a crazed young woman strode over and poured my pint of Ghost Ship over Richard's head, screaming, "You're such a bastard. You could at least have made some effort to contact me. I've lost twenty years of having a dad, but looking at you, it seems it hasn't been a loss, after all."

It was the young woman at the bar whom a few weeks ago Richard had tried to ingratiate himself with. So, this was Jess. I wasn't the father, after all. So much for immaculate conception. Witnessing her fury, I was relieved.

She had one of those nose rings often seen on bulls, and another one in her lower lip. The young woman wore dark makeup all the way around her eyes, and half of her head was shaved. It was a such an interesting appearance that I tried to move away, falling off my stool as I did so. She then glared down at me with an equal amount of utter venom, which I felt was a little uncalled for.

Richard seemed as confused as any man faced with this situation. In a moment of courage, I fished her letter out of my pocket and held it toward her. "I'm guessing this is you," I ventured, a little anxious, since she still held the empty glass like a weapon.

She paused, I held my breath, and Richard just sat there, clearly baffled.

"You put it in the wrong pocket," I said. "Richard didn't know."

I passed the letter to Headley, who read it with dawning understanding displayed on his face but, surprisingly, a glint of joy there, too. "I'd wondered why you didn't fall for my charm when I bought those drinks. I just assumed you were a lesbian."

"I *am* a lesbian."

"Well, that's wonderful ... darling," replied Richard with a wide grin.

She looked as if she were about to grind the glass into his face.

I stood up to leave, feeling this was a private moment for them. Well, relatively private if a whole pub full of gawping people were taken out of the scenario. I started putting on my coat, saying, "I think I'm going to let you two get to know each other. Richard, this is Jess. Jess, this, apparently, is your dad. Barnaby — I think we should hit the road."

Sadly for Headley, the movie moment, when he should have risen and embraced the daughter he never knew he had, was tainted by the arrival of two police officers in uniform, and behind them, appearing extremely uncomfortable, Inspector McAlister.

Richard was cuffed, arrested for the murder of his wife, and escorted out, leaving me, Barnaby, and Jess standing with the rest of the pub transfixed. Headley had been seen leaving the medium's home, and Saffron herself had finally plucked up the courage to go to the police and tell them that when she'd left her sacred grotto, somebody had come in and murdered her client. There was plenty of forensic evidence left in the room, Milky having failed to clear up much of the blood.

"I think perhaps, Jess, we should grab some chips at the Silver Cod, and I'll tell you about your long-lost father. He gets better with knowing."

As he was leaving, McAlister turned around, jogged up to me, and pulled out a folded piece of white paper from his inside pocket. He held my gaze as he slowly unfolded it, saying, "I'm doing a sponsored swim for the Rotary Club. Could you sign up, maybe for £20?"

"I don't have a pen ..." I started to say, then noticed in his other hand, of all things, a Plus Denario Orgasmia pen.

Leaving the inspector, Barnaby, Jess, and I headed to the Silver Cod, a few doors up the road. Outside the-fish-and-chip shop, yet again, stood the man in the hoodie, who I'd recognized as Rob Turney, the nurse from the surgical ward. He was engaged in a transaction with a passerby, which I was pretty sure was the selling of drugs. As we passed him, I just said, "We need to talk."

He glanced nervously at me, then shot a more terrified look as one of the customers in the Silver Cod emerged through the door. It was one of the giant Romanians.

Turney darted off, and Barnaby, Jess, and I strode into the Silver Cod to order takeaway.

# 40

# HUNTED

## DECEMBER 11, 2004

I'd previously described Ian Beaney as lacking both motivation and ethics, but in a very short space of time he'd secured a website — DrBeans4pets.com or something like that — and had found an innocuous molecule that could be fed to any animal "suffering" from Powel Syndrome. The molecule wasn't Orgasmia, which was too much trouble. Instead, it was a scientifically proven remedy endorsed by veterinarians, meaning Ian.

The best part was that so far it seemed to work. All Ian had done was import maple syrup from Canada and repackage it into small vials. But the owners of cats and dogs with nothing wrong with them swore by its efficacy.

On Saturday, I drove into town for a haircut. Upon leaving the barber, I immediately noticed a large woman with a small dog bearing down on me. There was no doubt she had me in her sights. I turned left and walked swiftly along Charles Street, then darted up the alley where the sewing machine shop was located. Nipping inside, I stood near the door, keeping an eye out for her. Sure enough, I saw her coming, and a few steps behind her was the Romanian behemoth. She marched straight past the shop, and once she was thirty yards away, I rushed out again, the shopkeeper unnecessarily inquiring after me, "Is that your long-lost daughter?"

Back on Charles Street, I took a look behind me: both of my pursuers had clearly seen me. The woman with the dog was too out of shape to get any farther and sank onto a bench. Meanwhile, the behemoth had broken into a run, so, by now terrified, I hurried into Colbourne's Department Store and barrelled straight through to the rear exit, not even daring to glance behind me. Crossing Main Street, I ducked into the library where I figured there were plenty of places to hide.

I hung around the biography section for about twenty minutes before calling a taxi. As it pulled up, I sprinted from the library and leaped into the back seat. The Romanian, I noticed, had spotted me, but as we drove away, he just stood on the curb, stared at me, and traced a finger across his throat in the universal language of murder.

When I arrived home, I locked all the doors and told Catherine what had happened. She said I'd imagined the whole event. *Maybe I did*, I thought.

# 41

# The Penny Drops

## December 14, 2004

I'd been asked to see a patient in the medical admissions unit who had a low white-cell count. He'd been brought in by ambulance after collapsing in one of the local pharmacies where he'd been buying medication for his dyspepsia. This was deduced not from his history but from the bottle of Tums he was clutching when he was brought into the admissions unit.

The urgent admissions unit was overflowing. Three extra beds were lined up in the corridor, with no beds on the wards to move even the sickest patients to. This used to be a Christmas season issue, but increasingly it was becoming normal for patients to sit around waiting for a bed to become available. Ten years earlier, the bed occupancy in our hospital was eighty percent. In other words, any specific bed was unoccupied twenty percent of the time. Now the mattress never even cooled down before the next patient occupied it. There was a story from Churchill Ward that one particular bed had hosted four deaths in a twenty-four-hour period.

I spotted two hospital managers with clipboards. Perhaps they were going to open up some more beds on Wellington Ward where two bays of six had been closed for cost savings. Oddly, they then started checking trash bins and writing feverishly on their clipboards.

One of them asked to speak urgently to the unit manager. The bin behind the main desk was non-compliant, and they demanded this be addressed urgently.

"Okay, I'll deal with it when things here are a little less hectic, probably tomorrow morning," the unit manager said.

"No, not tomorrow. This is priority one. It has to be sorted out immediately."

Once again, I thanked the system that created clear targets and goals to make the Health Service better.

Mary Taylor was on call that day, and as I approached the nurses' desk to get my patient's notes, she stopped me and said, "I wouldn't bother. He's completely demented." Then she returned to her own case. I wasn't sure she'd ever been someone I'd describe as warm, but her manner today was positively arctic.

I noticed her entry, which simply read: "Patient demented — unable to obtain reliable history." I glanced at a bed where a patient lay attached to various monitors. He appeared to be in his early eighties. The man was gaunt and grey and had the weathered face of a lifelong smoker, but his blue eyes were disconcertingly bright. He wore dentures carefully chosen to give him the smile of Donny Osmond circa 1975. Despite his incongruous Hollywood teeth, something about his very presence suggested wisdom from life experience notwithstanding the diagnosis of dementia. His name was Piotr Jacoboski. He caught my gaze and flashed his brilliant white smile, followed by a resigned shrug.

I called over a Polish orderly, Andreas Popovski, who happened to be in the unit, and asked him to have a word with Jacoboski, whose face immediately lit up as soon as he heard his native tongue. It took only two minutes for us to learn that the patient was visiting his son from Poland and had fallen ill in town while shopping alone. The only diagnosis here was that he didn't speak English.

Simultaneously, I had a moment of clarity. Jacoboski was no more demented than I was, but everything I'd seen with Professor Desmond Leech pointed to his obvious cognitive decline. Did he have early dementia? Was he still able to carry off his duties supported by his adoring team? Surrounded by the ambitious and the sycophantic, his condition could have been disguised for several months. With his junior doctors filling in and managing most of his deficiencies, they could help cover the tail-off in clinical performance, procedures that were considerably slower to complete than they'd been five years previously, the irrational bursts of temper, the disinhibited sexualized comments to young female nurses, the way he'd changed from immaculate dresser to a rather grubby, dishevelled appearance, and losing his sports car at the supermarket. It all seemed so obvious now.

I decided to have a chat with one of the psychiatrists, a Spaniard named Mateo Sanchez, who was in a constant state of smiling good humour and apparent horniness. Now there was a speciality I understood even less than choosing gynecology as a career. I guessed there were a lot of team meetings, plenty of coffee, and ginger nut biscuits. And it was the only speciality in which one could wear a sports jacket with corduroy trousers from Marks & Spencer.

There was something immeasurably tragic about watching a former esteemed colleague gradually diminishing in terms of his reputation. I needed to clarify that. *Esteemed* in the sense that he was admired and respected by many pharma companies and junior staff seeking good references. But still a totally conceited bastard consumed by hubris, who was rarely invited out to dinner parties since he was such vile company. I rather wished he'd retire, but the nature of an academic high achiever conspired against him as forty years of arrogance and success was prone to do.

I called the surgical manager, Danny Flowers, and relayed my thoughts. "You need to write Dr. Leech and tell him he'll be suspended from the trust," Danny told me.

"Me?" I queried. "When did this in any way become my job?"

He replied that I'd agreed to take the lead on this matter, which wasn't strictly fair, so feeling backed into a corner, I agreed to speak to Leech personally. Flowers had talked to me for forty minutes without mentioning the risk to patients. The only danger he'd cited so far was the reputation of the hospital should any of this story ever surface.

I decided to drop in on the professor in his office where I found him dozing. Gently, I woke him.

"Who the hell are you?" he snapped. "Get out of my office!"

"It's me, Brian Standish, Hematology."

"Well, I can't talk to you. I'm busy." He then made an effort to seem as if he had, indeed, been busy, which was somewhat implausible, since the only thing on his desk was the *Kilminster Journal* and an empty coffee mug with a picture of Princess Diana and Prince Charles when life appeared better for them. Or did they know even then, when the mugs were produced, that this wasn't a love made in heaven?

"Well, can we make an appointment for a chat?" I asked, failing to hide the tremor in my voice, for he still maintained an imposing presence.

"A chat?"

"Well, uh, yes, a chat," I stammered.

"About what?"

"I guess we were wondering if you'd thought about slowing down with your work. Maybe take a little break after all that's happened. I bet you were thinking about retiring soon."

And there it was. I had to tell him he was losing his mind. I couldn't do it, though, and ended up having a clumsy, unsuccessful informal conversation with Dr. Leech, suggesting he reduce his clinical workload and plan to retire. It wasn't received well. Indeed, he told me to bugger off. So I did.

I would have to do this in writing.

# 42

# DEATH BY EXSANGUINATION

## DECEMBER 15, 2004

The surgical ward remained unhappy about the increasing challenge of post-operative pain, but having seen Robert Turney outside the Silver Cod, I had a new theory. I decided to run a secret blood test on a Mrs. Smith, who despite receiving what ought to be ample analgesia, continued to complain of severe pain. I wasn't sure it was entirely ethical, but I checked for opiate levels in her blood. After all, she was on morphine for her pain. Sure enough, the result came back revealing no opiates.

So we were close to the root of the problem. Patients were getting more post-operative pain not because of Sir Desmond's technique but because they weren't getting opiates as prescribed. No wonder Mrs. Smith was in pain; she wasn't receiving any of the drug.

I'd already noticed that the link with patient pain was our sweaty friend, charge nurse Rob Turney. I felt the most likely scenario was that Rob was an opiate addict, on the basis that there were plenty of those in the health-care profession.

Knowing that the approach to such a crisis could sometimes be merciless, I planned to have a quiet word with Turney and see if I could persuade him to find a way to help himself with his problem. So, I sat there in the nurses' office trying to work out how to subtly approach him when the most unlikely thing happened. Turney actually approached me when the room was empty and asked if I could talk to him after work.

“I have to tell you what I saw,” he practically whispered to me. “I think I know what happened to Mrs. Headley.”

“I need to speak with you, too,” I replied. “I think you know why. You can trust me.”

Just then, Mary Taylor walked in, and Turney scurried out. “What were you guys plotting?” she asked.

Something about Mary always turned me into a stuttering fool. Unconvincingly, I denied any subterfuge.

Unfortunately, that day I had a basket-weaving class with Catherine followed by a guest speaker from the Morris Dancing Federation at the library. But I was free the following evening, and as I left the ward, I passed Turney a note asking him to meet me in my office at five o’clock the next day. Then I recorded this in my diary, too, just using his initials to keep everything confidential.

The following day, I hadn’t forgotten that I was meeting Turney at five. We had a small treatment room along the corridor from my office where we did bone-marrow biopsies or blood transfusions. As I was passing at 4:30, there was quite a commotion in the room, so I popped my head in. The nurse who ran the treatment unit was yelling something into her phone. Every person in the room was staring at a bed on which lay the whitest corpse I’d ever seen.

It appeared to me that he’d been phlebotomized, a procedure used for patients with too much hemoglobin in which we removed a bag of blood every few weeks. Normally, we extracted one or two bags. Lined up from abdomen to this corpse’s neck were seven bags of blood.

“Is this one of our patients?” I asked.

“No one was scheduled today,” the treatment unit nurse replied. “I don’t have a clue who this is. I’m really not sure what we should do. Should we call the police?”

We decided first to call the medical director, Dr. Leech, who was nowhere to be found. Then we contacted the medical manager and finally the police. After that, I jogged to my office to cancel my meeting with Turney so I could get back and support the team.

Rob hadn't arrived yet, so I left him a note on my door and returned to the treatment room, which by now also had the cardiac arrest team milling about. The team, unusually, had had the sense to realize that a body that had been totally exsanguinated was a poor bet for resuscitation.

Mrs. Macaron came by and asked if perhaps it would offer comfort to the deceased's relatives if we used the blood for tomorrow's operating list. She then scuttled off to order some refreshments, since her reaction to every crisis was to feed her colleagues and hope the solution presented itself.

Inspector McAlister was at the scene of the crime within thirty minutes of our call to the police, presumably because there were no sports on television at 6:00 p.m. on a Wednesday. Within ten minutes, I was arrested for the murder of Robert Turney.

Before being bundled into the squad car, McAlister grabbed me and said, "Before you go, sonny, I wonder if you'd care to sponsor me. We're raising money for presents for the officers' children."

I began to protest that sadly I had nothing to write with as McAlister waved a ballpoint pen under my nose.

# 43

# Freedom at Last

## December 17, 2004

The jailer came down this morning and stared disbelievingly at the two full notepads in which I'd written my account to date. From suppertime the night before and throughout the evening, I'd churned out my thoughts. Now that I considered them, they were a little disordered.

I was offered breakfast. One would imagine with the tax we all paid I'd get at least a bowl of cornflakes and perhaps two rounds of whole wheat toast with butter and thick-cut marmalade. But no, what they gave me was a ham-and-cheese sandwich, suspiciously identical to the one I got the previous evening, though the bread was a little more curled at the edges. Politely, I declined and continued to write.

Three hours later, the same brusque fellow who had processed me the previous evening told me that I could go home. No explanation, no apology. I gathered up my pillow and notepads and strode up to the main reception where they refused my request to call Catherine and thus I chose to walk to my office in the hospital, which was four miles closer than home. I would call her from my office. Halfway back, I realized I'd left my lunch box at the police station. I doubted I'd ever see it again. As I entered the hospital feeling a little grubby and dishevelled, I met Mrs. Macaron, figuring I probably smelled like a thousand criminals.

"Dr. Standish, I've been on tenterhooks. I heard the police were letting you go. The inspector told me last night it couldn't have been you. Worry not, I'll spread the word around the managers so that you don't become a social leopard. To all intensive purposes, I gather they discovered the body had been dead for four hours, so you couldn't possibly have done it since you were in clinical the whole afternoon."

Strangely, our CEO seemed to know more about the case than I, the accused, did. But at least it sounded clear that I was off the hook. However, if she knew this last night, why had Inspector McAlister kept me locked up all evening? Something else to add to my list of complaints.

I left the CEO and hadn't walked more than twenty steps when I saw the pathologist Rashid Chopra, another notoriously idle man whose post-mortems were limited in scope to what he could do in fifteen minutes, at which point he lost interest, such was his lack of academic zeal. He was excited to tell me that Robert Turney had, indeed, been exsanguinated using large-bore needles, one in each femoral artery. Preliminary testing revealed high levels of benzodiazepine sedatives in his blood, so he was probably dozing as he slowly bled out.

As I'd recorded in my account last night, I'd imagined that the most likely reason for Turney's death was related to either him stealing drugs from the ward, or something to do with what seemed to me like a gang working out of the Silver Cod. I made a mental note to let the inspector know my thoughts when I saw him next. It occurred to me that the large lump of a Romanian who seemed to be the persuader in the organization must have shown considerable skill inserting the needles and filling the blood bags. It seemed such a pretentious way to kill someone. I would have thought that an accidental fall from a high window was more in keeping with the Romanian way of dealing with undesirables. And why would they want to frame me for the murder?

# 44

# OUR DINING CLUB AGAIN

## DECEMBER 19, 2004

Two days later, Sunday, it was our turn to host the Economy Dining Club. It was bad timing. I had too much on my plate, and Christmas was just around the corner. Richard Headley had been released on bail and insisted on coming alone. He seemed worryingly unfazed to hear that the body in the foundation of Morris Furniss's extension was his wife and that he was the only suspect. So far his main observation was that there was no soap in the laundry room.

"How are you feeling about things?" I asked Richard.

"Well, much as I wanted her dead, I didn't kill her. She was driving me nuts. To be honest, I'm fairly sure she had Dutch boy fingers. She was always creeping off with various girlfriends."

"Sorry, Dutch boy fingers?" I asked, though even as I posed the question, my brain had computed the answer. Richard carried on listing Therese's faults, and I could only wonder at a man whose wife lay in a mortuary while he planned his next conquest.

We had a relatively small house, so we'd been forced to erect a camping table at the end of the dining room table, along with some deck chairs, leaving five of the guests sitting in the worst position to dine. I put a bottle of wine at the point where the two tables met, whereupon it immediately toppled over, glugging wine onto the white skirt of Jennifer Handy, wife of our local obstetrician. Considering Jennifer, I often wondered what it was like to be intimate with a man who spent his life ferreting around down there and pictured a box of gloves on the bedside table.

The evening started inauspiciously until Jennifer's husband, the gynecologist William Handy, appeared in the kitchen and rifled through the drawers, searching for a dessert spoon, which when found, he used to taste the beef casserole. Then he added salt and pepper while Catherine watched, disbelief on her face. I knew from experience her expression heralded imminent fury.

Quickly, I ushered Handy into the living room where inevitably he began to regale the guests with his latest vulva-vaginal anecdotes, which held no surprises, since they'd all been told several times before.

His partner was an aspiring opera singer who seemed to start most sentences with a normal voice but somehow finished as Tosca. The first time she did this was charming; the fifty-third time less so. I believe we were supposed to be impressed. Instead, I just wanted to find a handle to pull to open a trapdoor through which she'd whoosh with a final shrill cry, never to be seen again.

William was telling us about a patient with a syphilitic chancre on her stoma, a story I'd heard many times before, which I knew would end with the comment "She liked a bit on the side." I'd already headed back to the kitchen before the punchline was delivered.

Dessert was a simple apple crumble and custard, one of my favourites. "This reminds me of my childhood," I said. "My mum always made the best custard."

Catherine was clearly unhappy about my comment. "Oh, so you don't love mine? What's wrong with it?"

By 11:00 p.m., all guests except two had left. Alec Doyle and his wife, Moira, showed no sign they'd noticed the others had departed. Alec because he was barely conscious lying in the hall clutching the same whisky bottle he'd arrived with, with about an inch left. Moira because she was outside our back door vomiting onto what she thought was a compost bin but which was, in fact, a plastic trunk where we stored the children's toys.

"How do we get rid of them?" asked Catherine.

"I think we just go to bed," I replied.

The following morning, I served them their breakfast and drove them home.

It was my birthday, and as was traditional, there was a brief calculation of what lay behind and what lay ahead. Like a million others celebrating their birthdays today, I vowed to live every day as if it were the last. Catherine asked me to go to the recycling centre to get rid of cardboard, and thus my first day of the rest of my life began somewhat inauspiciously. The rest of my life continued with me spending twenty minutes sitting on our garden bench with a sharp twig trying to scrape dog poo out of the tread in the sole of the new shoes I'd bought earlier. I never really liked them after that. Tomorrow I'd live as if it were my last day. Today was already too far gone.

# 45

# SHOOTOUT

## DECEMBER 20, 2004

This was my last day of work before stopping for Christmas. It was only Monday, but I had the rest of the week off, so I spent most of the time in my office doing administration paperwork. Finished that, I went up to leave some tins of biscuits on each ward — Marks & Spencer of course, because I wasn't a cheapskate. As I returned to my office at about five o'clock that evening, I could smell a familiar stench of fried food and cigarettes. Initially I assumed it was the odour of my clothes from the mattress in the jail cell, but I soon discovered I was wrong.

From the corner of the room stepped the Romanian bouncer from the Silver Cod. The same giant who was always sitting in the takeaway exuding threat and evil and who had followed me through town.

A few things were certain about the colossal East European: he was dark, huge, mean, foreign, and planning to kill me. That wasn't paranoia on my part. There were several clues. The first was the murderous expression on his face. More convincing was the fact that he was holding a revolver aimed at my chest. The final clue was when he told me he was going to kill me.

"I'm going to enjoy watching you die, Dr. Starfish."

I was surprised that he didn't have much of an accent. "It's Standish," I corrected him.

His bulk was between me and the door. There was no escape.

The only weapons I had close to hand were an Orgasmia paperweight, an Orgasmia-branded pad of Post-it notes, and a ballpoint pen with Plus Denario written in gold. I picked it up and noted the other side said Orgasmia, too.

He saw me reaching for the paperweight, chuckled, and took a step backward. His shoulder caught the edge of the bookcase I'd erected only a week earlier. Catherine had warned me I was no carpenter. She'd also suggested that putting eighty copies of my novel *Fatal Medicine* in a box on the top shelf was a bad idea. The shelf gave way, and the box containing my unsellable first book toppled forward onto the shoulder of the Romanian hitman, who let loose with an oath in a surprising British accent. As a reflex, his right arm came up to protect himself and he accidentally fired his revolver, shooting off his nose and a piece of skin from his forehead. Immediately, I noted damage to the panel in the drop ceiling, which would take months to get replaced owing to the onerous process involved filling out forms for the hospital maintenance department.

I hurled the paperweight at his face, missing by about two feet, then threw the pad of Post-it notes at him as I bolted for the door. I was still two feet from the door when it burst open to reveal Wanda, the sister of the murderer Jeremiah Foch, brandishing a shotgun. With no hesitation, she fired both barrels, slamming two cartridges of pheasant shot at the gangster assassin. Amazingly, despite the fact that they appeared to strike him full centre and created quite a startling wound, he was far from dead.

The man staggered from my office, shoving Wanda aside, and lurched down the corridor, only to be tripped up by Mary Taylor coming the other way. Was she out to kill me, too? The thug dropped his revolver as he fell, and it skittered along the floor. He turned his head as he lay there to see Mary wielding a fire axe she must have pulled from the wall. There was no doubt from her expression that she could employ it effectively if he moved. Meanwhile, Wanda, with surprising agility and speed, bolted off in the opposite direction. I gathered later that the last image of Wanda was of her squeezing her full frame into a Fiat 500 and leaving the hospital grounds at high speed.

"Call security, Brian," said Mary in a calm, clipped voice, but I just stood there. "Now!" she added loudly.

I rushed back into my office to call for help. When I re-emerged, Mary was crouching and talking to the failed hitman. It almost looked as if she was squeezing his nose and covering his mouth.

"I'm just checking his airway," she explained.

He'd lost a considerable volume of blood and was close to death or already gone, I thought. Strangely, no medical emergency team had arrived yet, apparently because the woman on the switchboard had directed them to my original office, unaware that I'd moved two years earlier.

"He's dead," Mary said.

She might have told me the weather would be warm today, such was her lack of emotion.

"He said he wanted to confess to the murder of both Robert Turney and Therese Headley. Apparently, Therese had witnessed some drug transactions outside the Silver Cod, and he'd been ordered to kill her."

Mary stared hard as if daring me to contradict her testimony. She was still clutching the axe. I figured she must have been holding it before she could possibly know what was taking place in my office.

It struck me as a little odd that in his dying moment the hitman had revealed so much so quickly, but this certainly would be music to the ears of Inspector McAlister whose last day before retirement was today. He'd be able to triumph in his final hours on the job, finish the paperwork, and get home in time for the darts final on BBC Two.

# 46

# Christmas

## December 25, 2004

Christmas, the season to be merry. *Falalalalaa!*

We were hosting this year, meaning my mother with Percy in tow; Ian, Grace, and their children; and Harvey and his boyfriend whom I'd grown to despise. Harvey's previous partners tended to be taciturn and macho, but his latest, Salvador, was flamboyantly gay. Everything was drama, his pink-cardigan-clad arms flying around.

Harvey's boyfriend had bought us a CD of Peruvian pan pipe carols I grudgingly inserted in the CD player. It was as terrible as I knew it would be.

"I love it," chimed Catherine.

Christmas Day was followed by a week in the south of Spain with Catherine's friend, Emma Blenkinsop, her husband, David, and their family, who were pathologically happy like a TV advertisement for oven chips or a trip to the theme park Alton Towers. For completeness, I observed that family fun parks with roller coasters and adults in costumes featured on my no-go list, having been tormented by a group of American children singing what a small world it was, after all, on a grey, rainy trip to Disneyland Paris that had ended with me arguing with a petulant Frenchman dressed as a chipmunk who had inherited a dominant set of genes instructing him to be as obtuse as possible when conversing with the British. The kids had each bought a Disney Princess outfit at vast expense that we left in a washroom somewhere before even departing Disneyland.

Emma and David's most infuriating habit, other than being pathologically happy, was to teach their children the words to every musical written in the past century, so it was no surprise they were singing something from *Seven Brides for Seven Brothers* in the coach taking us from the airport to the resort we were to share for the next week.

As if things couldn't get any worse, Emma proposed, "Brian, you, Catherine, and the kids should choose a musical and sing one night this week."

We flew home the day after New Year's. My mood was rock bottom, and then just like that, everything improved. Every so often when life felt dull and miserable, something truly wonderful happened to remind me of the joys of creation.

Today was particularly noteworthy because Maggy Furniss, who had always seemed a quiet, timid little thing, knocked at our door and asked if we could pop around for afternoon tea with Nancy, our immediate neighbour.

I quickly consulted our list of available excuses. "I'm not overly sure Morris is going to be pleased to see us," I ventured.

With a wide grin, she replied, "Don't worry about Morris. He's dead."

I was at a loss for words. How did I say I was sorry for a loss when I felt like letting off celebratory fireworks?

She explained what had happened. As she spoke, I realized, with a vague sense of pride in the sheer audacity of Maggy Furniss, that she was retelling a story we'd heard from one of my colleagues who was discussing the perfect crime with Richard Headley. Maggy had been there, sans Morris, at a Christmas party when Morris was being interviewed by the police after the bodies mysteriously appeared in his garden.

The essence of the plot was that the coroner on the small Caribbean Island of St. Augustine, Grant McKay, preferred rum to working, so much so that he always had his first glass sitting on his verandah watching the sun rise.

Grant had perfected the art of total indolence but somehow managed at ten each morning to overcome his inertia and struggle the two hundred yards from his home to his small office adjacent to the rear entrance of the tiny hospital, just next to the doors through which the cadavers of the recently deceased made their way if the death was deemed suspicious or unexplained.

Under some sort of maritime law, if somebody died aboard a cruise ship, the death came under the jurisdiction of the next port of call. On St. Augustine, there hadn't been a single autopsy for seven years, and Grant could deem a death natural even if a hatchet was buried in the back of the skull.

A natural death could be processed in twenty minutes. There was a further bonus that McKay owned fifty percent of the crematorium, and an extra death potentially paid any debts owed to the St. Augustine rum distillery.

Maggy told me excitedly how Morris had died suddenly in their cabin and how his corpse, still dressed in a black leather thong connected by a silver chain to his right nipple, had been discovered by her when she returned from the slot machines.

I didn't ask if there was an empty glass nearby, or how she'd smuggled aboard the poison I suspected he'd consumed. However, I did recall her talking to Richard Headley, who was still discussing his thriller with people. Hemlock had been mentioned.

"In the end," said the grieving widow, "I had to leave his ashes in St. Augustine. It meant less paperwork for me and saved my having to pay for extra baggage allowance."

"I'm so sorry for your loss," I finally blurted.

"No, you're not. He was a vile human being. The last three days of the cruise without him were my best time in thirty years. Oh, did your mother tell you she was on the same cruise with some old army type named Percy?"

"It's a shame you didn't save a little hemlock for him, too," I said.

She smiled. "I don't know what you could possible mean."

January 4 in the new year was my first day back at the hospital, so I finally managed to pin down a time with Desmond Leech to talk to him about hanging up his scalpel and accepting retirement, something I dreaded because I knew it would likely end badly.

On the drive in to work, the roads were empty. Most sensible people had taken a couple more days off after New Year's. I reflected on how well things had turned out in the past four months.

The gangsters had moved out of the Silver Cod, and the original owner had bought the business back for half of what he'd sold it for a year earlier. It turned out they weren't Eastern European at all. Instead, they were actually members of an organized crime family from Birmingham. My mother would have described them as unsavoury.

Milky Norm was serving the fish and chips and was back to his normal self. He'd been through a revolution and no longer claimed ever to have been the Milky Bar Kid. However, he was insistent that he'd been in a baked bean advertisement in 1983 and had also performed the stunts on a well-known chocolate commercial that had been rerun around Christmas.

His mother, Saffron, was no longer a medium. She'd finally found her vocation as a sex therapist and already had a client, Richard Headley, who was struggling to keep up with the demands of his new belle.

Headley had made up with his new daughter, Jessica. He'd finished grieving for his late wife and had recently become engaged to Jessica's twenty-two-year-old roommate, who seemed besotted and not fazed by a thirty-year age gap. Clearly, Richard hadn't shown her any bank statements, for there was little else I could imagine she was attracted to.

Morris Furniss was dead, I thought with a grin. Probably dust in the wind by now somewhere in the Caribbean. And the world still turned without Mark Stone rippling his muscles at me.

Mary Taylor would ignore me if I ignored her. I was still sure she'd killed Richard's wife. Harvey distinctly recalled her crashing into him outside the Silver Cod, causing him to drop his sausage and chips. Mind you, after he'd returned to buy a new battered sausage, he also claimed to have been crashed into by Headley rushing out of the same door only five minutes later. I figured some things were best left alone. As far as the police were concerned, they'd found the murderer, albeit dead by the time they'd discovered him. Case closed.

I wondered if Mary had killed Rob Turney, too. Had he seen her entering Saffron's home before Therese was killed? Or was it the Birmingham drug dealers who used the fish-and-chip shop to launder money?

Ian was as poor as a church mouse. Sometime after the Christmas holidays, his wife, Grace, had announced she was leaving him. His initial joy at not having to do the deed himself was followed by horror when he accessed his offshore accounts to find them empty. His receptionist had disappeared off the face of the earth, though we were to learn later, not before transferring some of Ian's missing millions to his ex-wife.

Auntie Jean was doing well. In fact, she said she was coming to stay with us next week. I wanted to ask her about the photos I'd found in her room, though she might wonder why I was poking around in there.

The only remaining weight on my mind was having to talk to Desmond Leech. I still wasn't sure how this had become my job, but I wanted it done this week. It had dragged on far too long.

# 47

# The Solution

## January 4, 2005

Sir Desmond was standing outside my office when I arrived, looking impatient. I was impressed that (a) he'd found my office and (b) he'd remembered our appointment. Then I noticed his wife sitting in a chair thirty feet away, smiling up at me.

We entered the office and both took a seat. My mouth was dry. Not sure how to kick everything off, I fiddled with my free Plus Denario pen with the Orgasmia branding and tried to work out how to begin. Leech appeared disgruntled. Then the way forward became clear to me.

"I gather you've been feeling a little fatigued lately with brain fog and some muscle aching," I ventured. The last part was a guess, but I reckoned most men who made it to sixty-five must ache somewhere. "And I suspect you're getting occasional tingling and dropping things. Perhaps you haven't been feeling as happy as you used to."

Leech nodded sadly. To my surprise, he agreed. "I guess age is catching up with me."

I ran through a few more generic non-specific symptoms and concluded, "Desmond, I believe you have Powel Syndrome."

To my surprise, he seemed relieved. "I knew there was something wrong with me. But in my job you can't show weakness. Well, son, what can you do for me?"

"As it turns out, I know exactly what to do. You only need to do two things. First, you should stop working. You can't possibly continue to operate when you have such a severe case of Powel Syndrome." I reached for a small box in a desk drawer. "And second, you must take one of these tablets per day."

He stretched a hand out for the packet of pills.

"Fifteen milligrams daily," I said, passing him one of my free samples of Orgasmia.

# AUTHOR'S NOTE

However familiar some of these characters may seem to the reader, all are entirely fictional, and I apologize for any coincidental similarity to real humans.

Yes, I know there are loose ends. That's because this book is like real life — sometimes things don't immediately make sense. But luckily, eventually being a trilogy, I suspect things will become clearer. For example, where has Wanda Foch gone? I'm not sure. Was Richard Headley really innocent? He's such a charmer he might have gotten away with murder. Mary Taylor, too: was she a mass murderer or, in fact, just very misunderstood? And those photos in Auntie Jean's room in the care home …

Nobody would take the wrong kidney out, would they? Well, yes, as it happens, all over the world. Swabs, gauze, surgical drills, and blades are left inside patients a couple of hundred times per year in the United Kingdom despite rigorous checklists and procedures. Operations performed on the wrong patient, or the wrong site, occur in most hospitals one or two times per year on average. Medication errors happen far more frequently, and most are never confessed to.

These largely avoidable errors are known as "Never Events." If interested, I point the reader to the paper "Common General Surgical Never Events: Analysis of NHS England Never Event Data" (see pubmed.ncbi.nlm.nih.gov/33693752). Never Events aren't confined to my fictional hospital in Kilminster or indeed to the United Kingdom. They occur worldwide.

In Canada, I refer the reader to "Never Events for Hospital Care in Canada: Safer Care for Patients, September 2015" (see healthcareexcellence.ca/media/eceoshdc/never-events-for-hospital-care-in-canada.pdf). In this framework, I was struck by the authors' comment: "Never events do not imply blame; 'never' is a call to action, not a demand or an attempt to shame mistakes."

The wrong kidney event wasn't actually solely the fault of Dr. Desmond Leech, though the tendency to ride the wave of hearsay and blame we always see in large organizations sometimes prevents reviewing systemic processes that allow Never Events to occur.

I remain sure that Dr. Leech suffers from early dementia. Eminence in life is no protection from dementia, though high intellectual level can make early detection difficult as people learn to cover up the obvious early stages. An important aspect to consider with our belligerent professor is the *change* in his usual behaviour and functioning. For example, the surgery that, say, two years earlier he could do without any problem now takes him longer and seems more of a struggle. He has challenges with word-finding and can't remember the names of the surgical tools of his trade. When he requests a scalpel, he asks for "the tool you cut with." This is known as nominal aphasia.

Desmond was always curmudgeonly, but now has a frightening temper, using words he'd never have uttered a decade earlier, including *runc*. He used to be immaculately turned out. Now he has fried egg stains on his silk tie.

I maintain he isn't a bad doctor and isn't negligent. Real "problem doctors" often show behaviours that have roots in medical school, or as trainees, that have never been addressed. Most countries are realizing they have to develop processes for addressing the fall-off in performance that occurs with age.

I now realize why Leech blanked out Brian in the grocery store carpark. It was because he had no idea who Dr. Standish was. Perhaps a surgeon is a little bit like fresh fish and fighter pilots. There's a point where they begin to go off. I suspect my senior colleagues won't like me writing that. Clearly, there's a balance between the experience of having seen hundreds of patients and the inevitable decline in endurance, eyesight, and psychomotor function.

In the United Kingdom, most doctors retire by sixty-five, whereas in North America one can be forgiven for attending a medical meeting and feeling one is sitting with the cast of the movie *Cocoon*. For example, in Canada, sixteen percent of the medical workforce is over sixty-five compared to twenty-three percent in the United States and just five percent in the United Kingdom.

Less forgivable is the lack of handwashing, a crucial component of infection control. It's hard to believe that health-care professionals fail to wash their hands before and after patient contacts, though the challenge of finding a washbasin to perform the task is greater than might be imagined. I reviewed data in my home country of Canada. The Health Quality Ontario audit of handwashing is public information and easy to find (see hqontario.ca/System-Performance/Hospital-Patient-Safety/Hand-washing-in-Ontario-hospitals-by-hospital-care-providers). Hospitals across Ontario were surveyed, and adherence to the handwashing in many of them was below sixty percent.

Another introduction to the challenge can be found in the article "Twenty-Four-Hour Observational Study of Hospital Hand Hygiene Compliance" (see pubmed.ncbi.nlm.nih.gov/20850899). The authors reveal that health-care workers across the board were unable to meet the standard. Doctors were the worst. Visitors to the hospital rarely washed their hands. In short, there's no shortage of data on our lack of ability to follow the most basic principles of infection control.

VOMIT is a real acronym describing the problems that arise from our use of modern imaging. Forty years ago, if a patient had abdominal pain, a doctor would take the patient's history and then perform an examination. Nowadays, a patient is probably on the way for a CT scan before he or she knows it. And that's when the incidental cyst of no clinical significance can start off a cascade of further tests and procedures.

Hemlock contains coniine and some similar poisonous alkaloids and is poisonous to all mammals, particularly its seeds and roots.

Victims fall asleep and gradually become unconscious until death occurs a few hours later. In the spirit of sharing, Europeans introduced hemlock to Canada. I think I spotted a book on plant toxicology in Richard Headley's office.

The pharma industry clearly isn't as bad as described … or is it? Sadly, much of the fictional account of persuading doctors to "advise" the industry is completely true, and the baffling way in which groups and subgroups of patients are massaged to present data in the most positive light is also common practice. Most doctors have a rudimentary grasp of statistics, whatever they may claim.

If the reader remains in doubt about the way Big Pharma behaves, try this website: violationtracker.goodjobsfirst.org. In addition, here is a phrase from Sergio Sismondo's devastating book about the drug industry, *Ghost-Managed Medicine: Big Pharma's Invisible Hands*: "Drugs are just molecules with data attached."

Smuggling horse semen isn't a flight of fancy. Am I an expert about this? No! So apologies for the woeful lack of facts and believability, but I had to find a way for Ian to continue his unscrupulous life on the moral low ground.

Under the Importation of Embryos, Ova, and Semen Order, 1980, it's unlawful to import equine semen without a qualifying health certificate. European legislation on chilled and frozen sperm has been in place for many years to tackle the illegal trade. During the 2009 horse-breeding season, the British Equine Veterinary Association described a number of incidents concerning the importing of uncertified semen into the United Kingdom. A U.K. Department for Environment, Food & Rural Affairs spokesman said: "The horse industry has a responsibility to use only semen in artificial insemination of mares that has been collected and stored in accordance with the regulations."

I wonder if Ian and Darren were the inspiration for other criminals at the time, but I suspect not because they weren't chilling the product adequately. I don't believe the dairy industry could be used to carry out the aims of malefactors. Nonetheless, I've occasionally eaten some pretty foul yoghurt.

I apologize unreservedly for any inaccuracies in the book, albeit acknowledging it's largely ridiculous and total fiction.

Brian will be back soon. Ian will rise again. But Catherine will always rule the roost.

# Acknowledgements

I acknowledge the considerable expertise of my editor, Michael Carroll, who deserves an award for his patience dealing with a confusing word salad and turning it into the second part of the Kilminster Trilogy. I thank my patients for making my job into a non-stop forty-year roller coaster of fun and laughter. And mainly, I thank my family for being constantly ridiculous, led by Caroline, whose resilience and support show how true companionship helps us navigate life's uncertainties and challenges.

www.ingramcontent.com/pod-product-compliance
Lightning Source LLC
LaVergne TN
LVHW091139080826
845145LV00008B/2198

* 9 7 8 1 7 7 1 8 0 7 6 3 0 *